Michael Brophy

Sketches Of The Royal Irish Constabulary

Michael Brophy

Sketches Of The Royal Irish Constabulary

ISBN/EAN: 9783741193101

Manufactured in Europe, USA, Canada, Australia, Japa

Cover: Foto ©Andreas Hilbeck / pixelio.de

Manufactured and distributed by brebook publishing software
(www.brebook.com)

Michael Brophy

Sketches Of The Royal Irish Constabulary

SKETCHES

OF THE

ROYAL IRISH CONSTABULARY.

BY

MICHAEL BROPHY,

EX-SERGT., R. I. C.

BURNS AND OATES,

LONDON :	NEW YORK :
GRANVILLE MANSIONS,	CATHOLIC PUBLICATION SOCIETY CO.,
ORCHARD STREET, W.	BARCLAY STREET.

1886.

PREFACE.

———※———

A VARIETY of circumstances in connection with the service which I belonged to for a quarter of a century suggested such an effort as I now submit to the notice of the public and the Royal Irish Constabulary itself, *viz.:—*

Firstly, the peculiar political and social condition of Ireland at the period of the first formation of the force ;

Secondly, the military character that the organisation assumed ;

Thirdly, the heterogeneous character of the social condition of the classes from which the officers and men are drawn ;

Fourthly, the glaring grievances of the force, extending over many years, and its long struggle for redress ;

Fifthly, its discontent and almost total annihilation at one period ;

Sixthly, the state of public opinion touching its merits and demerits ;

Seventhly, its title of " Royal ".

Eighthly, its "Strike"; and, lastly, the stirring events

in which it has had to play a part in the chequered history of Ireland in latter-day times.

These are some of the chief motives which I fall back upon to justify the publication of the chequered matter contained within these covers. I have no pretensions to the possession of literary ability whatever ; and considering how the world now-a-days is inundated with oceans of literature from the pens of skilful *littérateurs*, such an admission must naturally suggest to the reader to say to me by way of advice and warning—

> "But why then publish ? There are no rewards
> Of fame or profit when the world grows weary ".

I must answer that I am careless and apathetic as to what may be the result, and it will serve my turn to finish the quotation of the stanza of which the above-quoted lines are part—

> "I ask in turn : Why do you play at cards !
> Why drink ? Why read ? To make some hour less dreary.
> It occupies me to turn back regards
> On what I've seen or ponder'd, sad or cheery ;
> And what I write I cast upon the stream,
> To sink or swim—I've had at least my dream."

MICHAEL BROPHY,
Ex.-Sergt., R. I. C.

EMILY COTTAGE, CARLOW.

CONTENTS.

——✳——

ROYAL IRISH CONSTABULARY.

CHAPTER I.

FORMATION OF THE FORCE.

In order to give the reader an idea of the curious composition of the Royal Irish Constabulary it will be absolutely necessary to take a cursory view of the social, political, and agrarian condition of Ireland at the period of the formation of the force (1823). About that time, and for some years later, Ireland might be said to be the "sick man" of the British Empire in the worst symptoms or rather phases of his illness. Trade, manufactures, commerce, and general industries of every kind were paralysed, eclipsed, and elbowed out of the world's marts by English competition; the majority of the landed proprietors were impecunious and bankrupt; absenteeism added its quota to the list of causes to which the decline of the nation may be traced; the creation of the Encumbered Estates Court was significant of the collapse of the landed gentry; the "fine old Irish gentleman" was ruined in the fine * (?) old Irish ways of extravagance and folly, and was obliged to have recourse to the subterfuge and expedient of the "court," mortgage, or rackrent, to extricate him out of the impecunious net into which he had fallen; the boasted eight millions of a population had begun to dwindle away,

* *Vide* "Ireland Sixty Years Ago," and Sir Jonah Barrington's "Personal Sketches".

to "grow small by degrees and beautifully less," until at length the "sick man" might be said to have received his *coup-de-grace* in or about the years '46-'47 and '48, by the failure of the potato crop and the terrible visitation of the cholera. The constitution that might have been instrumental in tiding the "sick man"* over the crisis, or more acute phases of his illness, had long since become prematurely moribund, and allowed itself to be absorbed into that of England.

Under such a condition of affairs, and when employment was so much needed by all classes, the force, as a natural sequence, was, and has been since its first embodiment in the year 1823, made up of a more curiously chequered and miscellaneous class of men than any other police force in the empire or perhaps in Europe.

It would almost appear that when that astute and most conservative of statesmen, the late Sir Robert Peel, aided and counselled by the Nestor of Irish chief-secretaries, the late Mr. Drummond (he who was the author of the dictum, "Property has its duties as well as its rights"), conceived and carried to a successful issue his pet scheme of a semi-military police force, for the suppression of crime and preservation of the peace of Ireland, he contemplated other designs and issues that might become evolved from such an organisation. The "sweet oblivious antidote" for the disturbed Ireland of that period, which, along with all its other "hastening ills," was diseased and honey-combed, so to speak, with all those mischievous secret societies, more the outcome of agrarianism than politics, that ramified everywhere among the rural population, rejoicing in the fantastic appellations of "Terryalts," "Shanavasts," "Corovoss," "Whitefeet," "Blackfeet," "Peep-o'-day-boys," "Rockites," "Ribbonmen," "Molly Maguires," *et hoc genus omne,* ministered also as a "sweet oblivious antidote" in a pecuniary manner to thousands of young men in Ireland, from the highest social grade downwards, inasmuch, as the constabulary scheme opened up a door of employment of a very

* I do not apply this metaphor to Ireland in the sense it is applied to another European State.

desirable and much-needed character. One could almost believe that Sir Robert Peel, inspired by Mr. Drummond, seeing the pitiable condition of Ireland, and feeling that the powerful sister-country had a hand in bringing that condition about, determined on making some small restitution by creating employment of some useful kind, one branch of which assumed the shape of a police force twelve thousand strong. I put forward this purely as a hypothesis; and, putting it in plainer words, it speaks in this wise :—" Your industries, manufactures, trade, and employment generally have been absorbed, paralysed, cribbed, cabined, and confined by us, and we give you as some small restitution in lieu thereof an annual subsidy in the shape of a constabulary grant for the employment of your surplus and unemployed men of all grades ".

In attempting to give an insight into the various classes, grades, and condition before they "joined," of the men composing the rank-and-file of the R. I. C., the following analysis might serve to give an approximate idea. Beginning with the higher grades that circumstances compelled to "join" in the initiatory rank of the force, and descending the social scale, it will be found that what I shall, for want of a better, term a "leaven" from the various *strata* of the Irish people go to make up the whole of that body of men whose transcendent *esprit de corps* and magnificent physique have made them world-famous.

Serving in the ranks are to be found the sons and heirs of the embarrassed or utterly ruined landed gentry. Their fathers or grandfathers had taken mortgage after mortgage on the paternal estates, until at length they do not own as much land as would "sod a lark," and the young men of the family have to look round for a living. They have learned no trade nor occupation, they "do not toil, neither do they spin," and they naturally gravitate towards the constabulary. It just suits them for a few years, till the mortgage is redeemed, when they resign their appointments and resume their proper position in society. Some indeed, whose patrimony is swallowed up and irrecoverably gone, perhaps in the gulf of long Chancery suits, resolve to make the force their profession for good, and take their fallen fortunes in as philosophical a manner as possible.

As I write my eyes rest for a few minutes on Thom's *Directory* for 1885. I seek down its columns and find the following entry :—

"Echlin, Sir Thomas, Bart., son of Sir Fenton Ferdinand, 6th Baronet, and Mary, only daughter of William Kavanagh, Esq. of Grangebeg, Co. Westmeath. Residence—Commandant's Office, R.I.C. Depôt, Phœnix Park."

" The wizard Time " brings strange transformations everywhere, but one would think that in Ireland he had established the favourite scene and theatre of his mutations. To trace the cause which left the present possessor of a baronetcy, so old that nearly all similar creations at present in Ireland might be said to be of mushroom growth in comparison, only a simple sergeant of police, is but to give an instance of the mass of romance of the same kind which Ireland abounds with. The Echlins became, like other families of Anglo-Norman descent, when settled in Ireland, *hibernicis ipsis hiberniores*, in so far at least that they lost their paternal acres by combative litigation, either litigant adopting as his motto "No surrender," until the broad acres were swallowed up in the unfathomable " Charybdis " of Chancery, leaving not as much as would "sod a lark" for the rightful owners or their heirs. The bare expenses alone of a suit that dragged with all the " law's delay " its " slow length along " from the year 1827 till 1850 (twenty-three years), when it ended, were sufficient to swallow up more princely patrimonies than that of the Echlins—

> " Not to talk of fees,
> Bonds, and horrible mortgagees ;
> To say nothing of assignees, lessees,
> And an endless quantity more of these
> Uneasy things that end in ee's,
> That drain the wine-cup to the lees,
> Or, as mice at a round of cheese,
> Leave nought behind by slow degrees."

Sir Bernard Burke writes of this family in his admirable work, *Vicissitudes of Families :—*

"The Echlins have been settled in Ireland since the reign of James the First. The Right Rev. Dr. Henry Echlin, migrating from Stafford in England, became Bishop of Down and Connor, in Ireland, from 1613 to 1635. In the latter year he met with a violent death at Balrudery, *en route* to Dublin. His grandson, Sir Henry Echlin, Knight, was second Baron of the Exchequer in Ireland, and obtained a Baronetcy, 17th October, 1621. Baron Echlin's eldest son Robert represented the borough of Newry, 1695, in the Irish Parliament. He married Penelope, daughter of Sir Maurice Eustace, Knight, and sister of the Lord Chancellor Eustace. His grandson, Sir Henry Echlin, the third Baronet, died suddenly, 1799, when the title devolved on Sir James, the fourth Baronet, grandson of the Rev. Dr. Echlin, Vicar of St. Catherine's, Dublin. This gentleman married Jane, daughter of Cambré Echlin, Esq., by whom he had Sir Frederick Echlin, the fifth and present Baronet."

So far the *Peerage and Baronetage* (edition of 1849) presents a record of this ancient family, but beneath the surface there lies a story of melancholy interest not told in the memorial of the nobility. It is to be found in the records of an equity suit. To pursue the details of loans and mortgages and their consequences, equity suits and bills of costs, though of all-absorbing interest to the parties concerned, would be an ungrateful task, and anything but an agreeable intellectual treat to my readers. "The Pleadings" in the dreary cause of Thomas *v.* Echlin commenced in the Irish Equity Court of Exchequer in the year 1827 and ended in the year 1850. It is needless to go into particulars ; the litigation went on year after year ; the lawyers enjoyed it amazingly ; they chuckled and punned and cracked jokes about it. To them it was food and raiment ; to the Echlin family, death and destitution. Sir James Echlin expired under the torture, and his son, the fifth baronet, inheritor of the family estate Clonagh, in the County Kildare, witnessed the suit glide from the defunct Exchequer into the living gulf of Chancery ; and he lived to see it end there—his estate sold and himself a pauper !

Sir Bernard winds up his notice of the vicissitudes of the family by the following passage :—

"The Baronet's brother, Fenton, continues to reside at Kilmeague, deriving his support from his sons, very deserving young men, one a policeman, another a private soldier in the Life Guards, and the third a footman."

A good many years have elapsed since the publication of the *Vicissitudes of Families ;* the wizard Time gives another stroke of the enchanter's wand, and the title, which, by virtue of being conferred by Royalty, seeks out, like the sound of the *Lia-Fail*, for the direct heir, and finds him a sub-constable in the Royal Irish Constabulary. The fifth baronet, Sir Frederick, dying without issue, the baronetcy devolved on his brother, Fenton Ferdinand, father of the subject of the present sketch. Sir Fenton having passed away, in some years after the present baronet succeeded him, being the eldest son. In Thom's *Directory* for 1885 there is the following entry touching the sergeant-baronet and his family connections :—

"Echlin, Sir Thomas, Bart., son of Sir Fenton Ferdinand, 6th Baronet, and Mary, only daughter of William Kavanagh, Esq. of Grangebeg, Co. Westmeath."

"Brothers and sisters—Henry Frederick (1846), John (1847), Ferdinand George, William Thomas (1876), Bride (1864), Emily Marion, Martha, Emma Mary. Residence— Commandant's Office, R.I.C. Depôt, Phœnix Park."

The sergeant-baronet takes his fallen fortunes lightly. Naturally a genial Mark Tapley sort of man, he is eminently popular with all ranks of the force who may be thrown in contact with him. In his room are gathered, since his accession to the baronetcy, the *souvenirs* and heirlooms of his ancestors, the most interesting object being the sword of General Echlin, who fought at the battle of the Boyne. The walls are hung with family portraits, pictures, and armorial bearings of the Echlins. In a corner is a great oaken box containing the parchments, family records, and title-deeds of property, now irrecoverably gone from the name, in Wicklow, Galway, and Kildare.

In the introductory essay to *The Vicissitudes*, the Ulster King-at-Arms writes (p. 7, vol. i.) :—

"Across the Irish Channel the story is even more

significant. There is perhaps no part of the world where such violent and almost incessant internal convulsions have disorganised society and overturned all social happiness and prosperity as in Ireland. The attentive student of Irish history is wearied with the record of perpetual wars. From the earliest period until within our own memory that fine country was the scene of civil discord, and for more than ten centuries it can scarcely be said to have enjoyed fifty consecutive years of calm. As a necessary consequence the Irish annals present a series of the most striking vicissitudes; and there is scarcely a family or a seat that has not shared deeply in those feverish changes and calamities."

Having thus far cited the testimony of Sir Bernard Burke touching the condition of the Irish landed gentry at the time of the formation of the Constabulary and subsequently, I will continue my analysis of the curiosities of the composition of the force, but before doing so will narrate an amusing episode in which a sub-constable of the class just noticed and his officer were the actors.

Sub-Constable D—— was a scion of a family that were ruined chiefly by horse-racing, a veritable type of the "Squanders of Castle Squander"; and, clinging still in his altered circumstances to the "horsey" traditions and proclivities of his family, he used to utilise all the leave of absence he was entitled to in riding steeplechases, sometimes professionally and sometimes in the "gentleman's race," providing always that the scene of the events was at a safe distance from the county he was serving in. On one occasion he was riding in a gentleman's race, and coming in the winner, he was surrounded by a knot of gentlemen, who had won on his "mount," to congratulate him on his success. One of these was his own officer, who chanced also to be at the races on leave, and great was his (the officer's) mystification and astonishment to see his own subordinate—or at least a man so closely resembling him that the likeness was phenomenal—in such a novel position. Staring in blank astonishment at D——, the officer accosted him, and in as delicate a manner as possible questioned him on the matter. "Pray, sir, pardon me; but might I ask, as I've won a considerable stake on your triumph in this race, whether you have got a twin-brother, and if he is in the Constabulary? You resemble a man so miraculously who is serving with me that I'd almost swear you are he."

"And you would be perfectly right, sir," replied D——, laughing at his officer's dilemma; "I am Sub-Constable D——, your man *in propria persona*, and no 'twin-brother of his'. I belong to a family that held as high a social position as these around, but simply, like a good many more in the same category, we came down to be 'hewers of wood and drawers of water'. Like Mickey Free's ancestors, sir—

> "'Oh, once we were iligant people,
> Though we now live in cabins of mud,
> And the land that you see from the steeple
> Belonged to us all from the Flood'.

I have still, you see, the old *penchant* for a bit of 'cross-country work,' and I'm glad you won on my 'mount'; and honour bright, sir, I know 'mum's the word' about this affair——"

"Oh, certainly, certainly, D——; not a word." And the officer kept his secret, but could never refrain from giving an involuntary smile when he encountered the gaze of his subordinate at home in their district.

The next "leaven" might be classed as the waifs and strays from the professions, the "spoiled priests" coming first. They are generally the sons of well-to-do farmers, whose absorbing ambition is to place a son or two in the priesthood, and they strain all their financial resources to maintain them in college till the rubicon of ordination is past. Alas! man is not perfect, and many an aspirant for the sacred ministry is "not called," and is thrown back on his disconsolate parents. Not being originally intended or adapted to labour on the farm, these "fallen angels" are obliged to cast round for a living, and, as the needle to the pole, they gravitate towards the Constabulary. I remember once to have known a sergeant who came under this category, utterly and signally defeat half-a-dozen far-advanced divinity students in a literary encounter where Greek and Latin came on the *tapis*, much to their discomfiture and astonishment. *En passant*, it is a curious fact that a considerable number of men who were never intended for the clerical profession, and who joined the Constabulary and served some years, aimed for, studied, and diligently read up for the clerical examination, and eventually resigned their appointments to become clergymen of the churches of their respective denominations. Then comes a sprinkling of rusticated, or rather frustrated, students of the various professions; erratic youths whose career in the professions they have adopted is brought to a precipitate *finale*, and are thrown back on their irate *pater* or *mater familias*, who refuse to do anything more for them, and make the situation so hot that a way of living is absolutely necessary. The Constabulary is found to suit them to a "T," and so they join. Many of this class have by their own exertions raised themselves to the rank of sub or now district inspectors. The next class might be said to be the school teachers. The teacher, the usher, or monitor grows weary of the worry, drudgery, and irksomeness of his profession, and takes it into his head that the Constabulary is a haven that affords him an escape. He takes the initiatory steps for admission, and eventually finds himself in that Utopian seminary in the Phœnix Park. Many a young "sub" of this "leaven" has coached and ground up his own authorities, sergeant, head-constable, or even sub-inspector, preparatory to a competitive "exam.," and to a successful issue too. The next may be termed the tradesman leaven. The young carpenter, mason, painter, stone-cutter, plumber, etc., etc., considers the rifle and sword-bayonet far more congenial "implements" than these of his own handicraft, and to this category the author of these writings belongs. Now comes the shop-assistants, a large percentage of whom have concluded that to wear a handsome and smart, if not gaudy, uniform, and to "strut *en militaire*," is far more pleasant than to be confined behind a musty counter, deep in the mysteries of profit and loss. Now we have the most numerous class that furnishes the rank-and-file of the force, namely, the sons of the farmers. It occurs frequently that the farmer has a numerous family and cannot break up his farm to portion them off, so perhaps one, two, or sometimes three, of the younger sons have to choose between emigration and the Constabulary. The latter generally wins the choice, and thus the " Irish *Landwehr* "—if I might draw such an analogy—absorbs a large proportion of the farming class of Ireland. Then come the sons of members of the force itself, and sometimes a literary man appears, who, finding himself in that impecunious condition which is a tradition of his *caste*, is practical enough to choose a comfortable barrack room in lieu of a noisome garret in the purlieus of a city. Lastly, there come men who cannot well be classed, and who have not adopted nor learned any trade or calling, but who went to school till the day of their joining the force.

Having thus far attempted to give a synopsis of the composition of the rank-and-file of the force, we will take a step up into what I shall term the " Laputa " of the Constabulary and see who is who there. The result of the analysis will show that the "upper crust " of the organisation is, in an equal ratio, as chequered as that of the rank-and-file. In the first place, it will be necessary to remark that as Maynooth College is, to the mass of the Roman Catholic farmers of Ireland, a medium through whose instrumentality their sons are assisted into the priesthood, so is the Depôt, Phœnix Park, an *alma mater* to the sons of the clergy of the Protestant Church in Ireland to pass them on to the much-coveted sub or district inspectorships. At the period of the formation of the force, and long subsequently, the humbler ranks of the clergy of the then Established Church were almost as impecunious and straitened in their circumstances as in the days of Goldsmith, who tells us they were

" Passing rich on forty pounds a year ".

To them the Constabulary scheme was a " consummation devoutly to be wished," as it opened up a door of employ-ment, of a very desirable character, for their sons, the purchase system in the army debarring them from a chance of carving their fortunes with their swords in that direction. The next "leaven" in the "Laputa" of the force might be described as the sons of the middle-class landed gentry. These young men do not ambition the army, yet would like to play at soldiers, and taste, in a safe way, a little of the " pomp and circumstance of glorious war," and so they prepare themselves for the competitive "exam.," get a nomination, and, if successful, duly run the prescribed *curriculum* at the Depôt, and from this chrysalis state they emerge full-fledged district inspectors. Next comes a very considerable "leaven " from the ranks of the bank clerks of Ireland, also a fair sprinkling of Civil Service clerks. These young gentlemen, albeit with good, nay, almost brilliant, prospects of rising in the world of Mammon, are smitten with the charms of the semi-military life ; they become ena- moured of the handsome uniform ; the clang and tinkle of the district officer's sword and spurs as he saunters by the bank windows, or perchance rambles into the edifice itself, is to them the sweetest of music ; alas ! in too many instances, the music of the syren that lures them to their ruin, if, figuratively speaking, their heads are not screwed on in the right place. If the ruinously extravagant habits that prevailed in the army officers' mess system called for re- trenchment and reform from the commander-in-chief, what a financial precipice, comparatively speaking, lies at the feet of the young Constabulary officer, which he vainly struggles to avoid. His position is one that invites and allures him to spend beyond his means. It is part of his instructions and duty to cultivate a friendly intimacy with the gentry of his district and neighbour- hood, for obvious reasons of Statecraft, so that, as it were, he becomes a species of Government ambassador or diplo- mat to those people. If he attends their assemblies, parties, *reunions*, balls, dinners, and is on visiting terms, etc., he must be as profuse and "good" as they, and "give" in return. Now, in the name of pounds, shillings, and pence, how can a man do that on the limited salary alloted to Constabulary officers, good although it be, viewed

from another standpoint. The fascination and glamour of
high society has been in too many instances the "Charybdis
and Scylla" of, alas! many a promising young Constabulary
officer; and I remember to have seen no less than four or
five, as they succeeded each other in the same district headquarters station, cashiered for financial shortcomings.

But not to digress further from the subject proper,
I find that a large percentage of the cadetships fall
to the sons of rich retired merchants. These young
gentlemen have an aversion to the counting-house, albeit
their *paterfamilias* may have accumulated a fortune there;
excelsior is their motto. Perchance they have discovered that *caste* is still rampant in the army, and will
not screw their courage to the sticking point to face the
"stigma of trade," so a cadetship in the Irish *gendarmerie*
meets their difficulty. Then it has often occurred that a
candidate for the army or navy fails to pass the examination
for entry into these services, and falls back on our Utopian
institution, gets a nomination, and very easily passes the
rubicon of the competitive "exam.," which is not so difficult a feat as that of the two former services. At the period
of the first formation of the force there was a large proportion of military and naval officers appointed to sub-
inspectorships, and, according to the testimony of the late
ex-County Inspector Curtis, the historian of the force, these
gentlemen were a little too impatient and fiery of the
"law's delay" in the discharge of their duties. This was
quite natural, inasmuch as men long accustomed to wield
the arbitrary and despotic power which the "Articles of
War" and military usage allows, could never well adopt
the stoicism and patience that is required in those wielding
the civil power. *Vi et armis* was their established motto,
and as for a recognition of *Civis Romanus sum*, it was only
a mere myth with them.

As in the case of the rank-and-file, the upper crust of the
organisation has a "leaven" from the professions—civil
engineers, medical students, journalists, tutors from high-
class seminaries and colleges, etc., etc. Now come the
sons of Constabulary officers, who have a recognised claim

to compete for vacancies on account of the positions occupied by their fathers, and the services rendered by them to the State. Lastly, comes promotion from the ranks; eligible head-constables are lifted into "Laputa" if successful in the competitive "exam." which the inspector-general sets apart for their especial advantage. In concluding my attempt at an analysis of the composition of the force, metaphorically speaking the Depôt, Phœnix Park, is a powerful magnet which, like the adamantine rock in the *Arabian Nights*, or the adamantine bottom of "Laputa," attracts and draws towards it all the various "atoms" of the people of Ireland just enumerated.

It might not be deemed irrelevant here to offer a few brief remarks on one or two vexed questions which have evoked a considerable amount of controversy and difference of opinion, namely, promotion from the ranks *versus* the cadet system. There are two sides to every question, and often more. In all justice such positions should be the reward of those who have well earned them by long and arduous service, commencing with the very initiatory grade ; and no class of men could have so thorough a grasp of all the ramifications of the working of the service and its system and amenities than those who have begun at the foot of the ladder and graduated upwards. However, it would seem that the exigencies of the Constabulary system and design preclude the possibility of such a rule as exclusive and entire promotion from the ranks to district inspectorship. These "exigencies" might be deemed as savouring more of political design than any other consideration. It will be remembered by the reader that I have put forward a hypothesis in the beginning of this section of my book, that Sir Robert Peel had an ulterior design in calling into existence so large a constabulary force, and that it was to open up a door of employment for *all classes* in a country that had been cribbed, cabined, and confined in her trade and manufactures by England. Granting such a hypothesis to be a fact, it could not possibly follow that the force should exclude from its employment *all* but those making up the mass of the rank-and-file, but it should indubitably follow as a rule that the appointments should be confined exclusively to Irishmen of all creeds and politics, not because the force is essentially Irish, but because of the "exigencies" just stated. On the same lines of reasoning and argument it should follow that a full, fair, and equal "leaven" of promotion from the ranks should take place. If the "preserves" by right of the "ranker" have been invaded and to a great extent monopolised, he at least should get a fair share of the only and highest rank he can aspire to or attain, *i.e.*, district inspectorship.

In concluding these remarks, I should have mentioned that appointments to sub-inspectorships in one or two instances have been made in a manner special and distinct from the prescribed routine of nomination and competition. I knew one of these appointments to be given on the "field of battle," so to speak, for brave and meritorious action on an occasion when a gentleman's house was attacked by an armed band. The two sons sallied out, and although outnumbered dispersed the attacking party and arrested the two leaders. His Excellency appointed one of the two defenders to a sub-inspectorship.

It is strange that the Royal Irish Constabulary, since its first formation, and up to almost the present time, has stood in the rather paradoxical position of being the best praised and lauded and best abused and decried body in the empire. Being without a parallel in its semi-military organisation, with exception, perhaps, of the French *gendarmerie*, it would appear somehow that the world at large has been always in a dilemma whether to bestow praise or abuse. Notwithstanding, however, the many vicissitudes and ever-varying spheres of action in which the Constabulary have had to play a part in Ireland, which, metaphorically speaking, is the "stormy petrel" of the great empire, the force have, through good and evil report, maintained au unsullied *esprit de corps*, and withal an unshaken popularity among the people. But it is curious that as the barometer indicates the ever-changing phases of the atmosphere, so does the calm or agitation of the political atmosphere in Ireland indicate the coming hurricane of abuse or praise which by turns falls to the lot of the police. In times of peace and tranquillity the force is abused, lectured, and criticised ; doses of satire are administered through the medium of the press by all sorts and conditions of people who can write, and have taken the *cacoethes scribendi* against the police. The hostile mania even extends to the judges on the bench ; all the stereotyped and hackneyed phrases of disparagement are brought to bear on them, such as "Too military in their organisation," "Drones in the great hive," "Must be abolished or reorganised," "An incubus in the land," "Useless body," etc., etc. This phase is generally when the political barometer is down to its peace, zero, when the "stormy petrels" are only hatching and are not as yet on the wing with their offspring, and the country presents a superficial calm until a brief interim of years elapses, when the incipient organisations grow into dangerous dimensions ; the "petrels" have hatched their embryo *émeutes* into full-fledged plots, and the police are once more on the alert to suppress the "rising" with their usual promptness and success. Then come all the stereotyped phrases of approbation and praise—"Model police of Europe," "Finest body of men in the world," "Magnificent physique," "Admirable organisation," "Brilliant *esprit de corps*," etc., etc.,—in fine, Hamlet's ecstatic admiration of his species might be specially paraphrased to illustrate the exuberance of the praise showered on the force.

To go back to the period when the organisation of the Constabulary first took place, their "quarry" was the numerous secret societies that were rather the outcome of agrarianism than politics, such as the "Terryalts," "Whitefeet," "Peep o' Days," "Shanavass," "Corovoss," *et hoc genus omne.* For years the warfare was waged against these nocturnal disturbers and local terrorists, and a series of encounters, dignified by the name of "battles," took place between them and the police, until one great "engagement" for supremacy, a species of "Waterloo," which generally gave the palm of victory to the police, was fought, when the secret organisation collapsed and dissolved, ridding the country, where it ramified, of an inveterate pest and plague spot. The "battle of Ballynochthen" broke the power of the "Whitefeet" in their headquarters, the Queen's County. After quiet being restored to the provinces and districts where these societies prevailed, on their final eradication there came a long interval of tranquillity, and with it a great amount of adverse criticism of the Constabulary administered through the press, from the bench, and in Parliament, until the never-ceasing whirligig of time brought round the memorable *fiasco* of '48, and, like the fluctuating stocks, up went the reputation of the Constabulary, who were be-spattered with praise in an exactly equal ratio as they had been disparaged and decried before. When the rebellion of '48 was "knocked into a cocked hat" and peace restored, there came a long interim of tranquillity, and with it down went to zero the *status* in public estimation of the Irish *gendarmerie*. That semi-military body was the re-cipient of quite a hurricane of adverse criticism from all quarters. The papers teemed with complaining letters about the "inactivity of the police"; doses of satire were administered; editors of papers joined in the cry; "Too military," etc., "Failed miserably as a detective force," "Mori-bund body" "Must be organised on another scheme altogether," etc. It became quite popular and fashionable to decry and abuse the police in those days, and the mania extended to their lordships, the judges on the bench, who invariably introduced the popular topic of the "uselessness of the police" into their addresses to the grand juries at each assizes, so that "Orestes being pursued by the Furies" was an approximate simile of the conditions existing between the Constabulary and the public at the time alluded to. So persistent and hot was this *hue and cry* that the then Chief Secretary, the present Sir Robert Peel, like Laocoon defend-ing his children from the fangs and coils of the serpents, rose in his place in the House of Commons and defended the force in a heated speech, in the course of which he administered a rebuke to the judges, who, he said, "were disporting themselves attacking the Constabulary". This hint had the effect of causing a lull in the "pursuit of the Furies," at least as far as their lordships were concerned ; and it was certainly curious that one or two who had refrained from joining in the popular outcry, now, as if the Chief Secretary's action in Parliament was their cue, spoke from the bench in unqualified praise of the force.

The Fenian *émeutes* now came on, and it will be superfluous to descant on the amount or quality of the praise bestowed on the police.   Never before did their barometer register so high a degree of popular favour and sunshine as after the suppression of that rising.   The distinguished title of " Royal " (a circumstance unparalleled and unprecedented in any police force in the world) was bestowed by the Sovereign ; a rise of pay with unqualified praise was voted by both Houses of Parliament.   In fine, it may not be deemed extravagant to say that the policy adopted by kings to strengthen their dynasties by having little wars on hand is as applicable to the case of the Constabulary in those days, as in the time of Shakespeare and the author of " The Prince ". I never read " The Prince," but Shakespeare makes the dying King Henry the Fourth advise his son and heir to go on a crusade to the Holy Land to please his subjects—

> " Lest rest and quiet still might make them look
> Too near unto my state.   Therefore, my Harry,
> Be it thy course to busy giddy minds
> With foreign quarrel."

UNIFORM, GRADES, PAY, AND PHYSIQUE.

The only thing worthy of note about the uniform is that it has been, from the first formation of the force, modelled on that of the army, and follows in the wake of all the changes and modifications the military clothing undergoes, as do also the arms, accoutrements, and general equipments.   In the days of the provincial depôts, each province, being ruled by its own inspector-general, had a different style of uniform, modelled according to the fancy of its chief.   When the provincial system was abolished for the centralised organisa- tion which made the present depôt, Phœnix Park, the head- quarters for all Ireland, this diversity made way for a general uniformity in clothing and appointments. To the uninitiated reader I may here explain that each member of the force must, along with his uniform, be possessed of a good suit of plain clothes, as is the rule in all other police organisations. *A propos* of this it will be amusing to relate that some years ago a military officer who got the appointment of inspector-general was so mystified, puzzled, and annoyed at seeing the twelve thousand men he was appointed to command, having each a box full of civilian apparel, that when he could not get it done away with, he threw up his appointment in disgust, so impressed was he that he was still to rule a military body.

The officer who first set foot into the Redan, at the Crimea, was the late Major Esmonde, V.C. He was appointed to one of the inspector-generalships, and held it until an unfortunate accident in the hunting-field necessitated his retirement from the force; he was a popular officer in both army and police. Side by side with him in the Crimea was the Royal Irish Constabulary contingent, a considerable body of both officers and rank-and-file, who volunteered their services for the commissariat department, and who are all in possession of the two war medals struck after the termination of the campaign.

Colonel Wood, late ex-inspector-general, assumed the *rôle* of a great reformer, and did more to ameliorate the condition of the rank-and-file than any other man who held the position. Yet he was the recipient, on his retirement from office, of a greater hurricane of abuse from the same rank-and-file, through the medium of the press, than ever fell to the lot of any man in the same position. To add to this, there were anathemas "not loud but deep" muttered (*aside*), to use a dramatic phrase, by a certain section of officers after him, as bitter if not more violent and bitter than the *hue-and-cry* of the men. This may be traced to the fact that his reforms and general policy balanced equally in the production of good and evil to the force and the philosophy embodied in the great dramatist's lines—

> " The evil that men do lives after them ;
> The good is oft interred with their bones,"

is as applicable to his case now as in the days when it was written.

Colonel M'Gregor, one time I.G., had one anxiety, and it was that no religious rancour, difference, or ill-feeling should exist in the Constabulary,—a very laudable "anxiety" truly. Major Priestly was the " Rhadamanthus " of the service and the severest man that was ever inspector-general. " Fine him I fine him! fine him!" were the last words he uttered ere he " shuffled off the mortal coil "; the ruling passion strong in death. Sir Henry Brownrigge wrote a *Code of Rules and Regulations* for the guidance of the force, which might be only paralleled by the *Code Napoleon* itself, or by some of Draco's laws ; but strange to say it was easier to get access to the two latter codes than to Sir Henry's *Code* in all barracks.   Colonels Hillier* and Bruce let the Royal Irish Constabulary alone, considering perhaps it was safer and easier than to be tinkering at them as some of their predecessors had been doing, and receiving "more kicks than halfpence," to use a homely metaphor, for their pains. Colonel Wood's† case demonstrated that the lines from " Hudibras " was in some way apposite to the R. I. C.—

"Alas what perils do environ
The man who meddles with cold iron ".

Colonel Maude, who held the post once on a time, seemed to confine all his attention to the good order of the lock of the carbine, the then small arm of the force.   His manner of inspecting was simply this.   He took the carbine out of each man's hands as he went along and raised the cock to test the soundness of the mainspring ; he looked at nothing else, and his maxim seemed to be, at least so far as the R. I. C. were concerned, " Put your trust in God and keep

---

* The eccentric but astute solicitor, John Rea, pocketed the £100 he mulcted Colonel Hillier of by an action for false arrest provoked by insulting language. He (John Rea) at the same time pronounced Colonel Hillier the bravest man who ever held the position, who would pay a hundred pounds sooner than brook an insult from a mere civilian.

† He was forced to retire for "disobedience of orders" in Sergeant Maloney's case. His Excellency had one way of thinking, and Colonel Wood held "No surrender" as his motto.

your powder dry ". To my mind the man best fitted to hold the reins of the Irish *gendarmerie* should have a combination of the following qualifications. Firstly, to be essentially a civilian; secondly, to be a lawyer; thirdly, to have graduated from the ranks of the officers of the force itself; fourthly, to be cool-headed and to well understand the meaning of the Roman legend, or rather axiom, *Civis Romanus sum*, the civil rights of the Romans. That man has at length been found in the person of the present inspector-general, Andrew Reed, Esq., LL.D., and Barrister-at-Law.

On an analysis being made of the various grades in the construction of the service, it will be found that there is a relative or rather equivalent rank for nearly every grade in the army from general down. For instance, the following table may serve to give an approximate idea :—

R. I. C. ranks.		*Army ranks.*
Inspector-General	is equivalent to	General.
Deputy-Inspector-General	,,	Lieutenant-General.
Assistant-Inspectors-General (2)	,,	Majors-General.
Commandant of Depôt (*A.I.G.*)	,,	,,
County Inspectors	,,	Colonels.
Surgeon to the Force (*Co. Inspr.*)	,,	Surgeon-Major.
Barrackmaster (*Co. Inspr.*)	,,	Quartermaster.
Adjutant at Depôt (*1st Dist. Inspr.*)	,,	Adjutant.
Musketry Instructor (*1st Dist. Inspr.*)	,,	Captain (Musketry Instructor).
First-Class District Inspector	,,	Major.
Second-Class District Inspector	,,	Captain.
Third-Class District Inspector	,,	Lieutenant.
Depôt School Superintendent (*Dist. Inspr.*)	,,	Inspector of Regl. Schools.
Cadet (*at training in Depôt for Dist. Inspr.*)	,,	Ensign.
Head-Constable-Major (*at Depôt*)	,,	Depôt-Sergeant-Major
Head-Constables (*ordinary*)	,,	Sergeants-Major.
Head-Constable-Storekeeper (*Depôt*)	,,	Quartermaster-Sergeant.
Office-Sergeants	,,	Colour-Sergeants.
Head-Constable in charge Depôt Hospital	,,	Hospital-Sergeant.

R. I. C. ranks.		*Army ranks.*
Drill-Sergeants (*at Depôt*)	is equivalent to	Drill-Sergeants.
Armourer-Sergeant (*at Depôt*)	,,	Armourer-Sergeant.
Sergeant-Assistant-Storekeeper	,,	Quartermaster-Sergeant.
Canteen-Sergeant (*at Depôt*)	,,	Canteen-Sergeant.
Librarian-Sergeant (*at Depôt*)	,,	Librarian-Sergeant.
Sergeants (*ordinary*)	,,	Sergeants.
Acting-Sergeants	,,	Corporals.
Constables	,,	Privates.

CAVALRY.

Cavalry R. I. C. ranks.		*Army ranks.*
Riding-Master (*Dist. Inspr.*)	is equivalent to	Captain (Superintending, &c.).
Veterinary Surgeon (*Depôt Co. Inspr.*)	,,	Army Veterinary Staff Surgeon.
Head-Constable (*Depôt*)	,,	Sergeant-Major.
Rough-Riding-Sergeant (*Depôt*)	,,	Rough-Riding-Sergeant.
Farrier-Sergeant (*Depôt*)	,,	Farrier-Sergeant.
Sergeants (*ordinary*)	,,	Sergeants.
Acting-Sergeants	,,	Corporals.

BAND.

Bandmaster (*Herr Von Mannen*)	is equivalent to	Regl. Bandmaster,
Band-Sergeant	,,	Regl. Band-Sergeant.
Band-Acting-Sergeant	,,	Band-Corporal.
Band-Constable	,,	Band-Private.

I must qualify the last-named comparison by stating that, although in the scale of equivalent ranks the constable is balanced with the private soldier, he is not in the same social status. A constable of the R. I. C. is supposed to be, by his literary qualifications and position, equal to a non-commissioned officer in the Army.

As nearly all the officers, non-commissioned officers, and men who are in possession of medals and clasps for the Crimean and other wars, I will enumerate a few of the officers still in the service who have been in the imminent deadly breach, viz. :—

Samuel Thomas Gordon, Esq., Surgeon to the Force, *Zulu War Medal* (1879).

John William Gloag, Esq., V.S. to the Force (late Vet. Staff-Surgeon), *Crimean Medal, with Clasps* for Alma, Balaklava, Inkermann, and Sebastopol ; the *Turkish Medal*, the Order of Knights of the Legion of Honour, the Fifth Class of the Order of the Medjidie.

T. P. Carr, Esq., Co. Inspector, *Crimean Medal and Clasps* for Inkermann and Sebastopol ; also *Turkish Medal*.

James Cotter, Esq., Dist. Inspr., *Crimean Medal and Clasp* for Sebastopol ; also *Turkish Medal*.

Pierre B. Pattison, Esq., Dist. Inspr., *Zulu War Medal*, *with Clasp* for 1879.

As a curiosity of the rates of pay and allowances of the R. I. C. the following analysis will show how, step by step, the Irish police struggled for, and, tardy though it was, gained an equality with their English brethren by legitimate agitation. For instance, in 1848 the annual salary of the head-constable-major — a hard-worked official — was only £70, in 1866 it was raised to £80, in 1870 to £90, in 1872 to £104. In 1836 a head-constable's annual salary was £50, in 1865 it was raised to £61, in 1870 to £65, in 1872 to £83. A sergeant's annual salary in 1836 was £32, in 1848 it was raised to £36, in 1866 to £49, in 1872 to £72. A constable's annual salary in 1836 was £27, in 1845 it was raised to £29, in 1866 to £41, in 1872 to £59. A number of other classes and grades not enumerated went on an equal ratio.

Touching the uniform, the old full-dress of the officers was a gorgeous one. Whether it was this uniform, or the full-dress uniform that superseded it, that attracted the attention of the late Emperor Napoleon at a review, I cannot vouch, but I " will tell the tale as 'twas told to me ". To lead up to this incident I must refer to the connection of the Bonaparte family with Ireland. Thomas Wyse, Esq. of the Manor of St. John's, Waterford, afterwards Sir Thomas Wyse, Her Britannic Majesty's representative at Athens, was married to Letitia, daughter of Lucien Bonaparte, brother of the first Napoleon. The marriage took place in 1821, and Madame Bonaparte Wyse came with her husband to Ireland. They took up their residence at the family mansion, St.

John's Manor, where Madame endeared herself to the people by her generosity and profuse charity. There are a few anecdotes extant of her life in Waterford. Once when some of the snobs that Ireland *par excellence* abounds with endeavoured at some assembly to put a slight on her, to rebuke them she said with withering scorn, "I am the daughter of a King, the niece of an Emperor, and the wife of Thomas Wyse". Sir Thomas, who was the head of the ancient and illustrious house of Wyse, died at Athens in 1852. His son and heir by Madame Bonaparte Wyse is Napoleon Bonaparte Wyse, Esq., D.L. of Paris and Waterford. The late County-Inspector Wyse, whose melancholy death by drowning whilst out fishing on a lake occurred some years ago, was nephew of Sir Thomas Wyse, therefore first cousin to Napoleon Bonaparte Wyse. When a young man in the service, he, in company with a brother officer, went to Paris on leave of absence, taking their full-dress constabulary uniform with them. On the occssion of a great review of the French troops on the *Champ-de-Mars*, when the late Emperor was in the hey-day of his power, Mr. Wyse and his companion appeared in their uniform. The Emperor, noticing them, sent an aide-de-camp to inquire their names and nationality, and on learning who they were he immediately ordered them to be supplied with horses and invited them to join his staff, so that during the day, cheek-by-jowl with that brilliant throng of generals, marshals, foreign princes, etc., rode the two police officers, *officiers de la gendarmerie Irlandaise*, as they were called. There may be many constructions as to the reason of the Emperor's friendship towards them ; it might be merely courtesy, or it might be the name of Wyse, or it might be their nationality. Perchance the Emperor might have remembered the days of his adversity, when he was sworn in a special constable, and had done his regular beat duty in London at the time when the Chartists made matters hot in that "Modern Babylon". It is a well-known fact that on his first official visit to London in after years he took the Empress to show her where he had done beat duty.

In closing this section, a brief analysis of the system

of numbering, and what it will disclose touching the number of men who have passed through the ranks of the Royal Irish Constabulary since its first formation, may not be out of place. To the uninitiated it must be explained that each recruit on joining receives a number which he retains during his service. This number indicates that he is the last of the hundreds or thousands that have been enrolled *before him*, whether they are *in* or *out* of the service. If he retires on pension, or is discharged, or resigns his appointment, this number retires with him and becomes extinct; no new recruit can inherit it, until perhaps, after a long series of years a revision of the numbering takes place, when a new generation of men takes up the the old numbers from one upwards. For instance the highest numbered man in the service is now somewhere beyond 50,000, although there are only 12,000* men in the force. This indicates that since the last *revision* between fifty and sixty thousand men have joined the ranks of the Royal Irish Constabulary! Now, on inquiry, comparison, and calculation, I am empowered to strike an approximate total of the number of men who have been enrolled since the force was embodied in 1823; and, adding the number that joined before the last revision of numbering to the above 50,000, we find that 80,000 some hundreds Irishmen have donned the uniform—a very formidable latter-day corps if they could be got together again. *A propos* of this, it is a curious phase of life at the Depôt to note the many hundreds of persons, of various callings and from all parts of the habitable globe, who had in early life graduated in the *alma mater* of the Depôt, Phœnix Park, and who, returning after a lifetime, wend their way to the Park to revisit the scene of their first entry on the great stage of life. Some who have failed, perhaps in making headway in the world, and return broken down and disillusioned of the *el-dorados* they sought in foreign lands, look in through the Depôt gate as the *Peri* is represented wistfully looking through the gates of paradise that are barred against her; and albeit the music he hears, consisting of the

---

* I believe the strength is now 11,000; 12,000 is its normal strength.

roar of the commandant, responded to by the unearthly yell of the adjutant, if it be battalion drill-day, may be somewhat different to the "music" the *Peri* hears, still, it would be as sweet to him if he could get back again. The Depôt buildings form three sides of a quadrangle and enclose the finest and largest drill-exercise ground or square in the empire. Along with the vast portion allotted for the use of the recruits as squad-rooms there are commandant's, surgeon's, adjutant's, and officers' quarters; cavalry stables, and riding school, depôt school, hospital, magazine, guard rooms, store, sergeants' mess-room and bar, depôt restaurant or canteen, recreation room with library attached, where, if perchance, dear reader, your footsteps may lead you, I promise you you will be received with as warm a *caed millia failtha* as ever you experienced, from that most courteous and hilarious of librarians, my old and esteemed friend Sergeant Tom M'Garrel.

From time to time groups of three, four, and five members of all ranks have volunteered for, and been sent to various parts of the world to organise police forces on the model of the Irish establishment, and in every case the system worked successfully. Some few years ago a native Egyptian official was sent by the Khedive's government to learn the rudiments of the Constabulary system, for the purpose of modelling an Egyptian police force on it.

Touching the semi-military character of the service and all the arguments and controversies as to its incongruity and unsuitability to a purely civil body, etc., I shall give an unbiassed opinion, and it is, that no matter what prime minister rules Ireland, whether he be in London or Dublin, he will be powerless without the Constabulary, as they are a semi-military body. Disarm and reduce the strength of the police, and how will peace be preserved, not alone in Ulster, which has to be invaded annually, but all Ireland to boot? It is all very well in Dublin where no jarring elements exist, but let us take Belfast for instance—the social volcano of the empire—to show how utterly futile would be the efforts of a disarmed and weakened Constabulary to enforce law and order there.

The disbanded borough police were mere "effigies" or "lay figures," that were the butts for the sport of Belfast rowdyism. They had no power and were utterly helpless in times of tumult and riot. In those times it was amusing to observe that when a party of them would be ordered by the Mayor or Magistrates to go and quell any rioting that was going on, they invariably demurred, unless they had a party of Constabulary to go before them. "We'd be useless," they would say, "to go there, your worship, without a party of Constabulary. Give us the *police* to protect us, and then we'll go. There wouldn't be a whole bone left in our bodies if we went into that place." They said the truth, albeit they were all, with the exception of one solitary man, of the favoured creed, yet those unfortunate "Dogberrys" came in for any amount of ill-usage if they attempted to stem the tide of turbulence on the part of the "fierce democracy" of their own way of thinking. When the inevitable hour came that saw them superseded by the R. I. C., that force had actually to reduce rowdy Belfast to submission, and to law and order. There were districts the denizens of which boasted that no arrest for lawlessness ever dare be made therein, and in these places a series of battles took place, until the rowdy element was made to feel it was useless to oppose the iron power of the Constabulary.

It is sheer nonsense to talk of the non-detection of crime, and attribute it to the too military character of the force. No matter what character an Irish police assumes, the same story will have to be told regarding Irish crime; and in discussing this subject camparisons with the catalogue of English undetected crime will show that, on the contrary, the Irish police have outstripped their more "civil" brethren of the sister country in the detective line, especially in the case of atrocious murders. *A propos* of this, I shall quote some passages from a letter of mine, written some years ago to a Belfast journal in defence of the force, and which was one of a long series of "tilting" in the same vein, viz. :—

"In dealing with the subject matter as to the efficiency of our body as a detective and deterrent element against the commission of crime, it might be deemed invidious to draw comparisons between our establishment and those of other great centres of the empire. To attempt to analyse and give statistics of the work done by costly police establishments in London, Liverpool, Birmingham, Manchester, and other great centres would be a work of supererogation ; but I will instance the metropolis of England itself, where a grim catalogue of crime stands as a melancholy testimony of the signal failure of the police force, as a detective and deterrent medium. The long list of homicides, not to mention a host of crimes of lesser magnitude, undetected in the ' Modern Babylon ' is simply appalling. This might be very naturally attributed to the vast masses of a heterogeneous people collected into one centre ; but it must be remembered that the numbers and magnitude of the police force is commensurate with the population in an equal ratio as with us here in Belfast. Not for a moment attempting to allege that this inefficiency in dealing with the crime of the metropolis on the part of the London police arises from neglect, stupidity, or apathy, for most probably the men put forth all their zeal, intelligence, and energy, yet it cannot be gainsaid or disputed that serious and vexatious blundering must be added to failure in the detection of crime. If such things occurred here what would be said of us and of our officers by the London papers and by those who eagerly seek for materials to carp at our system in and out of Parliment? It is well known that the London papers are not prone to be over-critical or severe on their own police ; but when a gallant officer who had seen service in the 'imminent deadly breach,' and who now holds a high post in this same civil force, came in for a dose of satire in a cartoon in one of the comic prints, things must be at a low ebb. ' Look upon that picture and on this.' It is still vivid in the public mind, how some few years past, people were horrified at the recital of a series of atrocious murders, and abortive attempts at the same, in an adjacent province, which were wrapped in a cloud of mystery. It was not agrarian nor seeming robbery, but it would only appear as if some sanguinary devotee of Moloch or Bohwanie was thrown on these shores, and had commenced 'to run amuck'* in the orthodox fashion of his dreaded sect. No clue presented itself whereby the dreadful mystery might be unravelled, until suddenly Belfast awoke one morning to be startled into the belief that the murderers were in its midst by the desperate 'attempt' in Joy Street. M'Dade commenced his terrible career in Sligo, and marked his blood-stained trail towards Belfast, where he made that determined attack which, happily, was his last. His arrest, which, in all probability, averted many more murders, was made by a Belfast policeman, Sub-Constable Crooks, under somewhat curious circumstances. The sub-constable, who had been recently transferred from the town to a country station, was sitting in his day-room, when an irresistible impulse urged him to go and look out into the street, where he saw, just passing, two tramps whose faces he thought were familiar to him. Remarking to a comrade that there were two Belfast characters passing by, and that a mysterious suspicion had taken possession of his mind that they had been committtng some depredation, he rushed out after them and put them under arrest. M'Dade instantly showed fight, when a desperate struggle took place, the civilians coming to the assistance of the policeman, and the desperado was secured. We know the sequel."

There are some allusions in this extract that at the time I wrote it were well understood, but which now require explanation. The blundering I alluded to was, in one instance, the failure in the Great Coram Street murder case, and the unwarrantable arrest and detention on suspicion of a German subject, a doctor by profession. The arrest and conviction of M'Dade was one of the most extraordinary and singular character, and illustrates once more the truth of the saying, "Murder will out". M'Dade was a tramp who got a night's lodging in the Sligo Workhouse, and after he left a series of murders took place. No one knew him or where he went. Some short time after, one night in Joy Street, Belfast, a rap was given at the door of a loan-fund

---

* Among the Thugs or Phanseyars and Malays the exclamation is while running "Amok! amok! amok!" literally "Kill! kill! kill!" Boh-wanie is the god of the Thugs.

office, which was answered by the manager, who, on the instant of opening the door, was felled by a blow from an iron bar by a man who, with a comrade, attempted to rob the office. The manager, however, struggled so desperately that the perpetrators beat a retreat, and made good their escape no one knew where. Next day their arrest was effected, in the singular manner described, by Crooks, and they were confronted with the manager and fully identified by him. There was no suspicion of their being connected with the Sligo murders until a sergeant from the town-inspector's office thought he recognised the clothes on M'Dade answered to the description of those taken from the house of one of the murdered men in Sligo. The telegraph brought down persons who identified the clothes, and this clue led on to a discovery of the whole sanguinary career of M'Dade and his conviction.

Touching the discipline, which is maintained with much rigidity, there is an equal meed of reward for meritorious conduct and actions, and punishment for insubordination. The fines are very heavy, and disrating and dismissal is visited on delinquents with impartiality from the highest to the lowest rank. Along with medals of various kinds there is a peculiarly distinctive reward given for heroic and meritorious actions which is called a "chevron". It is a device wrought in silver, having the recipient's name engraved thereon, and is worn on the right arm, round which it is strapped by a patent leather strap and buckle, to which the chevron is attached. There are two classes of chevrons, first and second, this latter being sometimes termed a "badge" or "half-chevron". The chevron is much prized and coveted in the service.

There is a return in book-form issued every half-year, giving a list of the rewards and punishments meted out during the preceding half-year, with the particulars of each case set forth, such as dismissals, disratings, fines, reprimands, etc. This return is facetiously called by the men "The list of the killed and wounded," abbreviated to "The killed and wounded". It has a great effect on the *esprit de corps* of the service.

A propos of this same *esprit de corps* of a body of men
drawn from all classes and creeds of the Irish people.   I
have shown how many a Protestant, Presbyterian, and Metho-
dist clergyman and missionary have passed through the ranks
of the force ; and as to the Catholics, who form, in a large
preponderance, the mass of the men of the service, many a
promising young priest and budding pulpit orator, regular and
monastic, both at home and on foreign missions, are the sons
of district-inspectors, head-constables, and sergeants.   The
promoters of charitable and benevolent objects always find
a fruitful field for their appeals among the Constabulary, and
if I could attempt to give an approximate total of the amounts
of money subscribed from the scanty cut-and-dry salaries it
would astonish the reader.   I will instance that, in further-
ance of the laudable project for the erection of a memorial
church to the memory of the most transcendent pulpit orator
of modern times, the late Father Tom Burke, the Constabulary subscriptions amounted to, if my memory serves me,
upwards of £6,000.

In attempting to give an idea of the straitened means of
the Constabulary and its outcome, I have put together some
few particulars and specimens of what came under my own
notice concerning members of the service, certain of whom
I came in contact with, and what I experienced myself.
Taken as merely the collections of one man, what a vast
mass of the same kind must be left in oblivion ; for what I
submit is merely a few fragments to serve as a sample of the
whole, and will bear testimony to that *esprit-de-corps* which
buoyed men up under pecuniary difficulties and urged them
on to have recourse to their own exertions, ingenuity, and
talent, to supplement their slender means and keep themselves from debt rather than combine in organising a strike,
and thereby hamper their government and place it in a
dilemma.   The Constabulary have always had recourse to
legitimate means of ventilating their grievances, and have
avoided all reprehensible action, until absolute want compelled them to organise the hateful strike, and even then
their action was surrounded with prudence and expressions
of loyalty, and the Prime Minister apprised by telegram

beforehand. During the land agitation, which assumed all
the phases and dimensions of a civil war, the Constabulary,
as in every other social throe that the latter-day history of
Ireland presents, had to bear the brunt of the battle, were
harassed day and night, and at the end of the campaign
found themselves head and heels in debt. The Government
very considerately voted a sum that was calculated to recoup
and reimburse their bankrupt police; but through some
tedious routine or red tapeism the money was not forth-
coming, and the vote remained apparently a dead letter.
The men waited patiently for months and months, but no
tidings of the sum voted them were heard, and grave doubts
as to its *bona fides* pervaded the mind of the force, who then
at the eleventh hour, when

> "Hope deferred maketh the heart sick,"

detetmined on a strike. The particulars of that affair are
still too fresh, being so recent, to need recounting here. It
will suffice to say that the Prime Minister expressed himself
strongly on the matter as to the neglect in not forwarding
the money in time.

To go back to the old times of limited pay and curtailed
expenses, Heaven alone knows how men supported themselves when absent at assizes, races, elections, North, etc.
The period may have been weeks or months, prolonged
perhaps, if some untoward circumstance arose necessitating
their presence, to three, four, or six months. The writer
served in a county in the early portion of his service which,
from its contiguity to Dublin, and consequently within call
from headquarters, was utilised for all emergencies arising in
different parts of Ireland, conspicuously the North, for the
12th of July or 15th of August. I remember once starting
to a northern county on Monday and returning on Thursday;
next day, Friday, ordered off back to another county in
Ulster, from which I returned on the following Monday
evening, and was just *half-an-hour* at home when a third
order pursued me, by the medium of the telegram and the
mounted man at district headquarters galloping after me
my comrade, to start us back again to another point.

After this I never returned to my station, and never laid eyes on it since, being kept in the capital of the North from exigencies arising that necessitated the retention of a large contingent as an auxiliary force. Such a precarious and, so to speak, Bohemian species of life must necessarily be expensive, for the hand must needs be in the pocket at all and every call. In the old times sixpence and a shilling per night extra used to be the expenses given to cover an expenditure of at least three shillings. However, this has been remedied by substantial increases since, notwithstanding which, in cases of protracted absence from quarters, even this substantial increase dwindles into a mere *bagatelle* before the flight of money. Then comes the difficulty of the Royal Irish Constable. The officer in charge cannot advance any more money, and subterfuge has to be resorted to, to raise the needful cash. If there are watches on the straitened individuals, a kind "uncle" takes charge of them, advancing the needful cash in lieu thereof, keeping the "ticker" as a hostage of good faith until redeemed. Some write home to other and nearer relatives, fathers, mothers, brothers, or sisters, to forward the much wanted cash; others to comrades at home in the distant station for a loan, and if that is not available, orders are given to invoke the good offices of the avuncular relative there, provided he resides within call. Others, perhaps, imagining they have a literary talent, occupy themselves in their spare hours off duty penning poetry or sketches of some sort or another, and endeavour to dispose of them to editors.

Petitions, memorials, applications, and addresses in rhyme have been resorted to time out of mind, and the chief reasons for adopting this style would appear to be the superior power of the muses to soften human nature, no matter how obdurate or impervious to appeal it might be. Music and poetry have been invested by the poets of all ages with powers beyond anything sublunary, and thus we are told how Orpheus with his lyre could soften the stern Pluto to let Eurydice go back to earth again. The Odes of Dryden and Pope on the subject and the many all   an us Shakespeare abundantly testify to the transcend   am

Euterpe—and of course her twin sister Erato must share
the triumphs—over all others of the " Nine ".   And so we
have it that petitions, etc., in rhyme have been sent by
tenants to their landlords, servants to their masters, soldiers
to their commanding officers, and it is recorded that
criminals under sentence of death have rhymed the Sovereign for a reprieve.   I remember hearing of an instance
where, in the reign of King George the Fourth, a condemned
man named George King sent one praying for a reprieve :—

> " If King George to George King
> Would grant a long day,
> George King for King George
> Would for evermore pray ".

Let us hope that King George granted George King what
George King petitioned King George for.

Conspicuous among those who fall back upon their wits
in this mode are the men of the R. I. C.   Many an amusing
production of this kind has found its way to the inspector-
general, and I believe with success in nearly every instance.
I regret I have only one specimen to submit for the reader's
perusal, and it will serve as a guarantee of the quality of the
rest.

Sub-constable Waters was one of those brave, dashing,
adventurous fellows—a numerous class in the force—who
unfortunately balance equally in an up-and-down, see-saw
kind of way heroic and meritorious exploits with wild
harum-scarum acts of indiscipline ; so that the good they do
is negatived for their own advancement.   He was reduced
in the old times of small pay and curtailed allowances, a
very serious matter, and he memorialises for a re-instatement
to his former rank :—

QUEEN'S COUNTY,
VICARSTOWN, *14th of May, 1854.*

MEMORIAL.*

" With your permission, I beg leave to state
That much misfortune was my lot of late,

* I am indebted to ex-Head-Constable Williams, manager, Hammam
Hotel, Sackville St., for a copy of this production.

3

Which, if I may intrude upon your time,
Officially I'll strive to send in rhyme.
'Twas in October last, the thirty-first,
A cloud of sorrows o'er my head did burst,
When I looked up true happiness to taste,
Ere all my days in hardship I should waste.
A rural station then I had in charge,
Whilst all my duties I strove to discharge,
Between civilians and my party too,
Impartially, which all the gentry knew;
But, sir, alas! the thorny path of life
With disappointment has been always rife,
For, when I fancied all my acts secure,
A slippery stone beset my barrack door.
Though prudence tells us danger to avoid,
Yet silly man, unthoughtful, is decoyed
Into the snares which crafty sinners throw
For man's destruction, which I'll plainly show.
Upon parade, when I found all was right,
I placed on guard a man named Thomas Whyte;
Then two for duty with myself made three,
Marched off to do it, underneath you'll see.
To Timoleague the two with me went down,
To Petty Sessions in that little town;
Unceasing rain poured on us all the way,
Which drenched our clothes and caused us much dismay.
After the Court we could not leave the town,
For rain in torrents poured in fury down;
We ordered dinner at O'Leary's Inn,
And after dinner took a glass of gin.
One of my party, sir, named Michael Harte—
A comely lad, intelligent and smart—
Soon left the inn and rambled through the street,
Where he some idle strollers chanced to meet.
An argument they quickly did begin
At his expense, which they believed no sin;
Nor did they stop till they his feelings hurt,
Then knocked him down and kicked him in the dirt.
They did insult him and assault him too,
Without a cause, which everybody knew;
But why they did so I will here explain.
We fined them all, which caused their mental pain;

Their crimes were inconsistent with our 'Code,'
For cattle wandering on the public road ;
They concentrated then in a crowd,
They bawled, they yelled, they groaned, and whistled loud ;
They made a noise that Harte might not elude,
Till Sergeant Parr did on the spot intrude.
On coming up he ordered Harte away
Unto the barrack without much delay,
Lest he might have the bayonet for to use
In self-defence from malignant abuse.
On further search, sir, I was found within,
With Patrick Pickett at O'Leary's Inn ;—
For Paddy Pickett was the third man's name,
A young recruit who was not much to blame.
The Court was over about half-past three,
And it was six when Harte had parted me ;
Our station was just four miles from the town,
Where we'd have been had rain not yet poured down.
We then were ordered to the station house,
Where off I sauntered meekly as a mouse,
Where through our facings we went on the spot,
As Sergeant Parr said we had liquor got.
Poor Harte submitted, for he was in fault,
But I and Pickett out our battle fought ;
And to convince him that I was not in error,
I did an act which many said was clever :
To show the party that my hand was steady,
My eye quite clear and no way heady,
I told the sergeant to stand stately by,
Whilst I a thread put through a needle's eye,
Which I repeated ten times o'er and o'er,
Whilst all the men stood round the kitchen floor.
A nicer act was ne'er performed by man,
To prove one sober, though a simple plan ;
And to show my speech it was quite clear,
And of my memory he need have no fear,
I pronounced and spelt—mark this, please, sir—
' Belshazzar,' and great ' Nebuchadnezzar ' ;
Yet I admitted in my explanation,
Being wet and cold, I took a small collation.
Now it appears my efforts were in vain,

For I was told in language very plain,
That I'm disrated down to second class,
As well as Harte, who took his flowing glass ;
And though young Pickett mingled in the throng,
I'm glad to mention he had not been wrong,
For he was sober and as firm as I,
As he the sergeant's efforts did defy;
Yet he was fined ten shillings for the part
He there had taken with his comrade Harte.
But, sir, to you I dare not once dictate,
As you can fine, promote, and can disrate.
Alas ! my pay is now made very small !
My tea is spilt, my teapot got a fall ;
My coarse brown loaf unbuttered I must eat,
Whilst butter glistens on my comrade's plate ;
I'm punished sorely in another's cause,
Though twenty years I've served the Empire's laws.
I risked my life my fellow-man's to save,
I rescued many from a watery grave ;
I saved a boy in January fifty-one,
Near to the ground the coastguards watch upon,
When loud tempestuous billows did defy
The coastguards' boats or others to draw nigh.
My space is small, or I could largely state
Some meritorious acts I did complete
In North Tipperary, ere my transfer here
Amongst the ' Terrys,' without dread or fear.
Now, lest I trespass on your precious time,
Ere I conclude I'll mention still in rhyme
One single act, but one, I'll only name,
'Twas death or glory, victory to gain.
My comrade Flynn and I one rainy night
An armed party quickly put to flight,
And took their leader with a loaded gun,
Whom I knocked down and captured in the run.
With loaded arms I did firmly clasp
That ' Terry ' bold who fell beneath my grasp,
Whom we espied as we patrolled along,
On which occasion I got a half chevron.
I captured others, I could name a score,
Whose hands were stained by red agrarian gore.

I sent them cruising from the county jail
O'er the Atlantic with a reefed topsail.
I have been active in my country's cause,
In strict obedience to my Queen and laws.
On Howley's pages oft my name is left,
At Quarter-Sessions prosecuting theft.
What I have done 'tis loss of time to tell,
'Tis all quite equal, be it ill or well :
Alleged offences, be they great or small,
Might be forgotten after six months' fall.
Though I faced bullets at the dead of night,
And armed parties oft have put to flight ;
And though I braved the deep at Union Hall,
'Tis not remembered when I got a fall.
Unguarded actions oft produce offence,
But long reduction makes a recompense ;
And this great truth the Sacred Scriptures say,
' The just man falleth seven times a day ' ;
And as it is the sacred will of Heaven,
That restitution makes a sin forgiven,
Six months' reduction pounds, shillings, and pence,
I humbly hope makes ample recompense.
Now, in conclusion, one request I crave,
Emancipation for a wretched slave ;
I humbly ask the rank I held before,
Which I will keep unstained for evermore."

HENRY WATERS, 2nd S.C., 1161.

"Onwards haste, make no delay !
To Major Priestly get away !
Whose answer from the Castle gate,
I here in silence humbly wait."

MINUTE OF MAJOR PRIESTLY.

"Though the sub-constable has been five times reduced, yet he is
restored to the rank and pay of first-class sub-constable from the 1st prox.,
hoping he may study his own interest henceforward."

E. J. PRIESTLY, D.I.G.

Major Priestly had the reputation of being the severest
man that ever sat in judgment on cases of indiscipline, and

the most rigid disciplinarian that ever occupied his position. However, Rhadamanthus himself should yield to the redoubtable Waters's appeal ; even that one touching and excruciating line, " My tea is spilt, my teapot got a fall," would soften sterner men than either Rhadamanthus or Major Priestly.   The metaphor should touch the heart of prince and peasant alike.

The following beautiful little poem was written by Subconstable Patrick Stacke, a native of Comragh, County Waterford, who has since resigned his appointment and become editor of an American journal.   It is the only fragment I can produce of his literary compositions, and it was written by him on a sickbed, from which he concluded he would never rise ; but his foreboding did not come to pass, for he recovered, to be able in after years to "sling ink" in the States.   The poem is composed in a laconic species of metre intended to be suggestive of a person gasping out his last request on earth, and it is entitled—

" THE LAST REQUEST."

I.

" In a nook
Where the brook
   Murmurs by.
In the gloom
Of the tomb
   Let me lie.

II.

" At the head
Of my bed
   Place the stone.
All I claim
Is my name—
   There alone.

III.

" Let the green
Still be seen
   Where I rest,

Of the grand,
Dear old land
I love best.

IV.

" Should you pass
O'er the grass
Shed a tear,
O'er the wild
Mountain child
Sleeping here."

" KILCOLGAN."

Sergeant Richard Cronnolly, Irish scholar and *littérateur*, was a remarkable man of his rank and position in the force, and I rejoice that an opportunity presents itself in the scope of this book to revive and perpetuate, in some small way, his memory among the men of the Royal Irish Constabulary. He wielded his pen to supplement his scanty income in the old times of small pay and allowances, and he was well known to Dr. O'Donovan and other eminent Irish scholars, who held him in high esteem. When the old *Catholic Telegraph* flourished, under the editorship of W. B. M'Cabe, and when the great Dr. Cahill thundered in its columns, Cronnolly, under the pseudonym of "Kilcolgan," supplied weekly the subject-matter of the column devoted to "The Origin of Irish Names," so that his *nom de plume* was familiar to thousands who had no suspicion that the learned genealogist was a simple sub-constable (he was not then promoted).

His most ambitious literary attempt was a genealogical account of the Irish race from Adam down, two parts of which he had just completed when he fell ill. Sad to say, the "fell sergeant Death was strict in his arrest," and Cronnolly passed over to the majority. He was, during most of his service, attached to the Reserve Force at the Depôt; but, his health failing him, he got himself transferred to a county, where he succumbed to a lingering complaint. The first part of his work is entitled "An Historical Account of the Clanna Rory," descendants of Roderick the Great, Monarch of Ireland, in which he refers to himself at the end of his account of the O'Cronnellys thus :—

"The lineal descendant of Matudhan, Prince of Crich Cualgne, and of Donal of the Moor, holds the initiatory grade in the Irish Constabulary force".

DISCONTENT.

A variety of circumstances tended to produce in the ranks of the Constabulary an amount of discontent, unexampled in any other kindred organisation in the great Empire, or even in Europe; and it is most curious and extraordinary that this discontent never developed into that phase which was a thing quite usual in other police forces, namely, the hateful strike, until the eleventh hour, when that necessity, which has no law, broke down the barriers of the famous *esprit de corps* which had characterised the body from its first formation. "Rebellion, foul, dishonouring word," was ever farthest from the instincts and intentions of the force ; they always followed the rule of legally withdrawing from their contract with the Government, by resigning their appointments, and seeking in a foreign land the bettering of their condition, and, by so doing, making room for others of their young countrymen to try their fortune in the service. The Government, on their part, always reciprocated this fair dealing by allowing such men to rejoin if they found that the rose-coloured pictures of far-off lands and the prospects there were not what they expected. Many who resigned and emigrated to the Colonies, Canada, and America became disillusioned there, returned, and rejoined, better and wiser men for their bitter experiences.

The history of the causes which produced the great discontent alluded to, and which threatened the dissolution of the whole force, will add its quota to the singularities which distinguished the Constabulary from all other kindred bodies. It was a good many years after the first formation that the incipient germs of a discontent manifested themselves, which for years increased and crept on, until at length it arrived at such grave and alarming dimensions that a crisis was brought about that threatened the total dissolution of the force. The causes which led up to this may be traced to the following circumstances :—

Firstly, the tide of emigration was at its zenith ; glowing and attractive pictures of the glorious prospects that awaited the stalwart young men of Ireland were floating before the imagination of the force, coupled with the syren-like invitations of friends and relations already gone there to come to the new worlds—the Colonies, Canada, or America. Secondly, these " El-Dorados " had ten-fold attraction when the young men of the force reflected on their prospects in it—a very gloomy one at that time. It was all very well for the first few years of their service, until they began to look round and feel their strength, position, and prospects. The pay was at its minimum, and scarcely served to keep a single man, let alone a man with a family, and all incidental allowances in the shape of expenses for duty at assizes, races, fairs, elections, in the north, etc., etc., were in an equally curtailed ratio to the pay. Thirdly, the prospects touching the retiring allowances were as remote and problematical in the minds of the men as the discovery of the North Pole. They looked forward through a long, distant, and dreary vista of bondage-years undefined and illimitable, stretching up to thirty, and probably beyond it, if an *ordeal*, more dreaded than a service of ten years more at the back of the thirty, was not favourable to their retirement (I allude to the medical examination). Then the next reflection was, that the curtailed pensions were scarcely worth the long battle of life in the service and the risks to be run; to run the gauntlet, as it were, of the chances of dismissal and loss of service and of position, perhaps after a life-time of service, was always a potent factor in decimating the force of its best men. An ugly comparison was always dangling before the eyes of the Irish police in the far superior condition of their brethren of England.

These are some of the main reasons which produced that great discontent which characterised the force for many years, until at length a series of circumstances combined to make the service one of the best in the world. At the time alluded to, and stretching over a number of years, each of which produced a crop of resignations of the flower of the service, every post was laden with official documents, marked O. H. M. S., and enclosing hundreds of resignations to be laid before the inspector-general. Recruiting was pushed forward vigorously to make up for this " hemorrhage," but to no great purpose. The drain went on and increased, until it reached a crisis that became alarming. The in-spector-general of the time, Sir Henry Brownrigg, made representations to the Government, but nothing was done to stem the tide. The papers, notably the *Freeman*, devoted a series of leading articles to the matter; once or twice a-week the " Dissolution of the Royal Irish Constabulary " was the theme of leaders and sub-leaders, calling on the Government to step in and prevent such a catastrophe by some remedial measure. This state of affairs reached its climax, when one morning the inspector-general rushed up to the Lord-Lieutenant and, in utter consternation, laid before him a crop of three thousand resignations ! After this the Government paid serious attention to the alarming state of affairs, and something was done which at least left a nucleus that brought the service back to its normal strength. Most of the men that remained were not a jot the less dis-contented because they *did remain*, and those that could write kept hammering away through the medium of the papers throughout Ireland, ventilating the grievances of the force, so that the literature of the discontent of the Con-stabulary was as familiar as household words in every paper, provincial and metropolitan.

As an outcome of the long struggle of the force for its rights, as regards pay and pensions, there exists at present the most curiously unjust and anamolous condition of affairs, touching the rule regulating the scale of pensions. There was a Royal Commission appointed, in 1866, to inquire into the grievances of the force, and the action of the Commissioners in striking the rate of pensions left two different scales, a superior and an inferior one, or, to use a musical term, a "major" and a " minor," with an "interval"

of one day between them. The explanation of this curious
decision is as follows. All men, down to the last-joined
recruit, who were lucky enough to be in the force before
and up to the day the Commission set its seal and veto on
their new regulations, were placed under the superior or
" major " scale, and all men who joined *after* that identical
and mysterious day were under the inferior or " minor "
scale, so that a fruitful source of discontent was a heritage
of that movement to a vast number of men, who very
naturally must keenly feel the disparity of their prospects
in the distant future. Serving side-by-side with their more
fortunate comrades at the other side of the Commissioners'
" rubicon," doing the same work, serving the same number
of years, only a few days, weeks, months, or years of seniority between them and their rivals, they find themselves
entitled to a much smaller pension. The Commissioners
put forward very cogent logic for this arrangement, and it
was this—That having raised the standing pay in so sweep-
ing a manner for all newcomers, in contradistinction to what
the men in the service previously were in receipt of, these
new appointments should accept small pensions, whilst the
men who had been on small pay should be rewarded with
large pensions. In dealing impartially between the Imperial
Exchequer and the force, of course, this was fair dealing
enough, if men could see it in such a light; but it is not easy
for men to be so philosophic of a cold winter's night on the
side of a mountain on patrol.

With these few main facts as to the discontent of the
force, I will pass on to give some details of the exigencies
arising from the straitened pecuniary condition of the men
of the service, and its various outcomes, both at the time
alluded to here, and coming down to a recent period, when
the land agitation and its amenities produced in the force
the unusual and unprecedented expedient of a strike.

PHYSIQUE.

Before entering on a few sketches which I fancy might
come under the heading of " Physique," I wish to give a

few notes as a sort of introduction on sobriquets. Sobriquets are things quite as familiar in the R. I. C. as in the Army. I believe in the latter service there is scarcely a colonel or high-place officer who is not known by some sobriquet or another; some peculiarity, mode of drilling or inspecting, or conspicuous idiosyncrasy is ingeniously utilised for the purpose. There was one colonel—an Irishman—who from his peculiar manner was called "Bouncing Barney" by his men. He knew it, but did not dislike it in the least. In a good deal of instances the initials of the name do service for the sobriquet, and sometimes the Christian name is abbreviated. As a few instances we have "Tim Stiff," "Showldherem," "John the First," "John the Second," "Tommy," "Sam," "James L.," "Billey," "G. O.," "H. B.," "Th' Ould Hawk," "Paddy," "Big John," "John F.," "John T.," "The King of Liliput," "Rhadamanthus," "Ould John," "Henry A.," etc.

Touching the first two, "Tim Stiff" was the lineal descendant, in a direct line, of the chieftains and princes of a Milesian sept, and, inheriting the old Celtic pride, put on a manner which suggested "Tim Stiff"; he was a county inspector. "Showldherem" was a county inspector of the old school, and he received his curious nickname from his singular manner of inspecting a party of men on parade. When he ordered the head-constable or sergeant, as the case might be, to put the men through any movements in drill, he invariably prefaced every word of command of the petty-rank man, by an abbreviated order of his own, so that no *liberties* could be taken while *he* was there, and all movements should emanate from *him* as their fountain and source. "Now, then," he would say, "sergeant, put the men through the manual and platoon (*now "firing"*) exercises —shouldherem." *Sergeant*—"Shoulder arms". "Presentem." *Sergeant*—"Present arms". "Shouldherem." *Sergeant*—"Shoulder arms". "Supportem." *Sergeant*—"Support arms". "Shouldherem." *Sergeant*—"Shoulder arms". "Orderem." *Sergeant*—"Order arms," etc.; and here he went on in a running fire of "shouldherem, fixem, shouldherem, portem, chargem, shouldherem, unfixem, slopem, orderem, groundem, loadem, readyem, presentem, firem, advancem, retirem, foursem, leftem, rightem, rerum, frontem, squarem, doublem, haltem, dressem," etc. Now this curious mode assumed an intensely comic phase when some daring spirits in the ranks now and then added such orders as "kickem," "batem," "murdherem," "starvem," "smashem," "tarem," "crushem," and if the sergeant was unpopular "reducem"; the strangest portion of it being that "Showldherem" never seemed to take the slightest notice of this indiscipline in the ranks. Why "Showldherem" was selected for the sobriquet was because it occurred oftener in the words of command than any other.

"Big John" was supposed to be the largest man in the Constabulary, and he was also known as "Hercules". I shall select him to illustrate my notes on physique, and detail some incidents and episodes in his life. For this purpose I must take my readers back to a by-gone time. It was on the occasion· of the Queen's first * visit to Ireland—a halcyon time indeed for the young sovereign. In the first flush of life when no domestic bereavement had as yet cast its shadow over the royal hearthstone to cloud the morn of her wedded life; when the "suits and trappings of woe" were as yet unknown in the Regal wardrobe, the first visit to the "Green shores of Erin" went merry as a marriage bell. From Cove to the Capital was one ovation; north, south, east, and west were *en fete*. The festivities, ceremonies, receptions, levees, balls, reviews, investitures, etc., were all organised and carried out on the most splendid and effective scale; there was no stone left unturned to make this Royal visit a memorable one. Foremost in the programme was the holding of the great military review, when almost every organised body of men in Ireland was utilised to supplement the military display and give this "gathering of the clans" a colossal proportion and brilliant *éclat*. Two thousand men of the Irish Constabulary were selected from the *crème de la crème* of the force to take part in it.

* I may be in error here as my memory does not serve me. It is probable it was on the occasion of the second visit in 1853—opening the Exhibition.

No man under six feet high was eligible to proceed to Dublin for this purpose. In those times the stature of the men was at its maximum, so that indeed the flower of the Irish nation in physique was represented in those two thousand men of the Constabulary. To enhance the great average stature and make more imposing this splendid body, the uniform of the time was admirably suited; the full dress coatee padded to a miracle and fitting each man without a wrinkle; the shoulders mounted with the ornamental epaulettes, squaring up, and giving an additional width to the broad expanse of chest; the full dress cap of the period towering high and broad with its glazed covering and wide burnished brass chain reflecting the sun's rays; the Wellington boots of the time with their high heels added their quota to the *tout-ensemble* of that corps of two thousand men, which was unequalled on that memorable day. The small carbine with its burnished brass mountings, light and unencumbersome, seemed a mere plaything in the hands of the giants who quietly held them at the shoulder.

Now it so occurred that, as a necessity in the order of the great "march past" in which the auxiliaries took a part, the Constabulary were to bring up the rear, this arising from the fact that the police, being a civil body and not under the Articles of War, could not take precedence of any military body. That "march past" was a memorable one; for hours before that brilliant throng which surrounded the Sovereign and her Consort, there filed past the flower of the British Army, infantry, cavalry, and auxiliaries, running the gauntlet of keen criticism from thousands of observers, civil and military, foreigners and natives. All Dublin and his wife, with the four provinces, were there to swell the throng. At length the everchanging and interminable "kaleidoscope" of the army marching by was drawing to a close, and the last body, the rear-guard, is seen in the distance. The startling contrast in uniform and stature in what is now approaching to all that had gone before strikes the vast throng, and a strange murmur of surprise and curiosity is heard, which gradually swells to a shout of disapproval from the Irish portion of the assembly, the cause of which arises

from the idea in their minds that so fine a body should be
bringing up the rear. Her Majesty eagerly asks the Prince
Consort if he could tell her what strange regiment it is that
is now approaching, but the Prince seems as mystified as
everyone else ; questions are eagerly put on all sides as to
the identity of the curious two thousand; foreigners and
natives who were unacquainted with the semi-military organi-
zation stared in blank astonishment when told it is a body
of policemen who are approaching. On they came like a
wall, steady, solid, and ponderous, impervious and imper-
turbable to the sensation their appearance created. With a
march and tread as if one man, they made the ground
vibrate, and as they advanced the murmur of dissent and
disapproval rose high and loud among the Irish, especially
the Dublin section of the spectators, who imagined that a
slight was intended ; that instead of last they should have
have been first ; of course non-military people could not
understand that this was impossible. However, the men
themselves were well satisfied at the "position" they
occupied, for, aware of their own superiority in physique,
they were indifferent as to whether they were first or last.
Foremost, a giant among giants, "Big John" strode in the
van, the wonder of many a spectator on that day, and many
a facetious allusion to him was heard—"Hollo ! is this the
Colossus of Rhodes ? "—" One of the Titans," "Goliath,"
"Finn M'Cool," "Hercules, King of Clubs," "Arminius,"
etc.

Like most giants, "Big John" was as quiet and unoffend-
ing as a child ; he looked down on ordinary people in some
sort of a way as Gulliver is represented looking down on the
Liliputians, kindly and good-naturedly, and he delighted in
exhibiting his great muscular powers, which nature seemed
to have delighted in his case in combining with great size.
In his prime he never was beaten at any athletic exercise,
whether it was leaping, wrestling, running, weight-throwing,
etc. Indeed, there is a famous leap which is called after
him up to this day, as no man ever performed the feat but
himself. There was another famous leap which he performed in conjunction with a priest. It was to leap across

the locks of the canal, which are of course of uniform width throughout. The priest, a powerful man too, performed the feat but succumbed to the effort; he never recovered; " Big John" did it easily. His ribs were joined together from top to bottom, forming a species of cuirass to his breast, and his jaws and teeth were equally powerful, so that he could nip a nail in twain as easily as if he were using a pliers. His voice was in keeping with his great *tout ensemble*—a deep barrelly-bass-fee-faw-fum-I-smell-the-blood-of-an-Irishman sort of voice, that Lablache the great basso might envy, and he might have played the giant in a pantomine without "making up" for it. I remember well when he came to my station on transfer, and, curiously enough, he replaced " Billey," the smallest man in the service, whose portrait will be found elsewhere. I was a recruit at the time, and, being small and juvenile, he said to me in a sympathising sort of way in a broad Munster accent—" Take care, alannah, that I don't tread on ye; ye'd never recover if I did; and don't vex me or maybe I'd ate ye; I ate several; I never report a man at all; I caution him, and if that won't do, I put him down in a pot an' boil him an' ate him; I'm a giant," and he made a most hideous grimace at me. It was curious to observe the manner the two men, opposites in physique, "Billey" and "Big John," regarded each other. Billey, who had gone out on pension and was residing hard by the barrack, when he saw the Colossus that replaced him, hid his diminished head for weeks in the recesses of his house. He was seen indeed peeping out furtively now and then, and disappearing again if his bulky successor was about, as if awed and terrified; and indeed the metaphor put into the mouth of Brutus touching the pinnacle of power Cæsar had arrived at was literal in Billey's case—

> " Why, man, he doth bestride the narrow world
> Like a Colossus, and we petty men
> Walk under his huge legs," etc.

Having thus far attempted a "pen-and-ink" sketch of the biggest man in the force, I shall narrate in a new chapter a few amusing episodes in his career; not indeed anything of a character touching adventures with Blackfeet, Whitefeet, Terryalts, etc., with whom "Big John" had many encounters and "set-to's," for, not contemplating a project like this book, I did not note any of the many stories told by the great man.

CHAPTER II

STORY OF A SWORD.

"I have another weapon in this chamber :
It is a sword of Spain, the ice-brooks temper."
—OTHELLO.

IN the late County Inspector Curtis's *History of the Royal Irish Constabulary*, there is an allusion to the appointment to sub-inspectorships of a considerable number of military officers, at the time of the first formation of the force, and that those gentlemen were too fiery and impatient of the "law's delay," never adapting themselves to the amenities of their new position with any sort of philosophy. The old *militaire*, it is asserted, could never be brought to understand that the dictum *Civis Romanus sum* was a fundamental and unalterable principle handed down from the greatest people of antiquity, and revived and established in this empire by *Magna Charta*.

Such a man was Mr. Sub-Inspector D——, ex-captain of the line, who had served under the "Iron Duke" in all his Peninsular campaigns, and a true type of the high-handed, blustering, fiery old campaigner of the great captain's school. Although getting this civil appointment by way of a *douceur* to assist his pension, he eminently disliked the position, with its restraints, prosaic routine, its law-and-logic amenities ; and many is the time he chafed and fumed when he had to cave in to some snubs from their bewigged lordships at Assizes for not being more active in getting his men to keep order in Court and suppress noise. "Go down out of that box, and try to stop that noise in Court ; you'll be far better employed than perched up there," snaps some of their cranky lordships, and down goes the ex-captain-sub-inspector muttering anathemas, "not loud but deep," at the day he accepted a sub-inspectorship. *A propos* of this, I once heard a story of a certain judge, whose name was once familiar in people's mouths, who, presiding at an Assizes, saw a young policeman posted at a certain door in the morning, at midday, and in the evening, and suspecting that he had not been relieved for his dinner, his lordship beckoned him towards the bench, and asked if he had had his dinner. The young fellow replied that he had not. The judge then called for the officer in charge of the Court, and, when that functionary appeared, his lordship asked—"Have you had your dinner, Mr. Officer?" "I have, my lord." "And have you had breakfast and tea, not forgetting your luncheon?" "Yes, my lord." "I'll engage you have. Will you explain to me how it comes that this unfortunate young policeman hasn't been relieved for either dinner or luncheon, and it is now six o'clock? Go, sir, at once, and have him relieved; you should have done it before this; but you were too well employed at your hotel to attend to your duties in this Court. 'Tis well for you and many more that I'm not inspector-general."

But not to digress further from the subject proper of my sketch, Sub-Inspector D——'s temper was not the mildest, and once angered, his language, to say the least of it, was rather strong. No time, place, or presence had any effect in checking his ebullitions of wrath, and he ofttimes amazed the "going judge" by a volley of "selections" from his military vocabulary at some recalcitrant disturber of the Court. He had many souvenirs and mementoes of his campaigning life. One in particular was a famous Toledo sword, which was presented to him by a Spanish noble in recognition of services rendered to his son, an officer in the Spanish service, when wounded on the battlefield. This weapon was *par excellence* of Toledo's best and most artistic workmanship; the blade was a miracle of elasticity and temper; the devices and tracery were marvels of art, and the hilt was in keeping. Nowhere outside the famous city of the swords, not even in Damascus itself, could anything be found to rival this beautiful weapon. The temper was such that the blade could be bent till the point met the hilt, describing a perfect circle, and when released it rebounded to its original straightness, without displaying the least sign of the strain. The scabbard was also a work of art in keeping with the blade. "The Captain"—as he was generally called—took great pride in exhibiting his *bric-a-brac* collection, but above all this sword was the *pièce de résistance* to delight and astonish his visitors and guests. On ordinary duty his regulation sword was of course used, but on any occasion of importance or ceremony he invariably wore the "Toledo," especially if a "present arms," which necessitated the drawing of it, was to be given. It was something to witness him giving the word of command, "Present arms!" and drawing forth, with a great flourish and clang as it leaped from the scabbard, the glittering blade.

He was stationed for a good many years in Parsonstown, and the noble scientist, the Earl of Rosse, who was employed at that time on his great telescope, admired this sword very much. The Captain used to say to him triumphantly when, perhaps, a group of gentlemen had satisfied their curiosity—

"Eh, my lord, can you produce anything like that? You may bring the stars within measurable distance, but you cannot measure swords with me; your lordship can do wonderful things in your smithy and foundry, but you cannot rival my 'Toledo'."

"Why, Captain," his lordship would reply, "I haven't tried; who knows but if I tried I could outdo your 'Toledo'. We don't know what we can do, you know, till we try."

The love of arms is such that the Captain's mania for exhibiting his "Toledo" to friends extended to his men; and in his absence the head-constable, sergeant, or acting-sergeant, were wont to take their curious friends to have a surreptitious peep at the steel beauty, and do the "show-man" for their gratification, when the weapon, like an acrobat, had to go through a round of performances, the chief one being the "hoop-trick". One day in the Captain's

absence " Big John "—who was the district head-constable—
in exhibiting it to some friends, carried the point beyond the
hilt, and as the best of tempers is liable to be broken, the
sword suddenly snapped right in the middle, to the utter consternation of all present. Here was a disaster indeed, fraught
with dire results, when the choleric and irascible Captain
would have to be encountered over it. What was to be
done? or who could suggest a remedy? Toledo was in Spain.
The servants were horror-stricken, contemplating the prospect
of the little earthquake that would be experienced in that
house when their lord and master came to find it out.
There was another association with the sword which I
forgot to mention up to this, which made it doubly precious
in the owner's affections. It was handed to him by the
Doña Inez, the dark-eyed and lovely daughter of the Don,
her father, and the Captain looked upon it for *certain
reasons* as a present more from her than from her sire. Some
one thought of Lord Rosse; perhaps the noble scientist
could do something with it, and to Lord Rosse " Big
John " straightway went with the broken sword. He found
his lordship in his smithy, occupied in forging some important
part of his great telescope; and when he saw " Big John,"
whom he often utilised as striker, when some particularly
heavy piece of forging was going on, he said, " Hollo, head-
constable, here, I'm glad you've come ; I have a very heavy
piece of forging to do, and your sledge-stroke is worth ten
men's rolled into one."

In a few minutes the glowing and hissing metal is on
the anvil, and a shower of sparks from thundering blows
would give one an idea of Vulcan's smithy or the Titan's
workshop, for his lordship was a strong man too. When
the " heat " was finished his lordship said, as he called for a
basin of water to wash his hands :

" Well now, what do you want, head-constable? Some
document to sign I suppose."

" No, my lord ; I wish it was only *that* that I wanted your
lordship for ; it is something more serious," and he unrolled
from a piece of green-baize cloth the two halves of the
broken sword. " I am undone if your lordship cannot aid

me; I broke the Captain's precious Toledo, and you know how he prizes it."

"Oh, indeed I do," replied his lordship. "How did it occur?" and Big John detailed the manner it happened, whilst Lord Rosse examined the break.

"Well," said he, "I'll try what I can do with it. Come to me to-morrow evening at five o'clock."

At the appointed hour "Big John" made his appearance, and his lordship presented the sword to him seemingly as perfect as before it was broken and asked him to point out the break. No indication that the weapon was ever broken could be detected, until a magnifying glass was applied, and then was seen, what the naked eye failed to detect before, a thin white line which showed a dovetail of the two parts together. The white line was the "silver braze" which knitted them together. Big John's mind was now easy; he was profuse in his thanks to Lord Rosse, and returned forthwith and placed the sword in its resting-place in the hall of the Captain's house. Lord Rosse warned him that if the sword was bent there was a probability that the weld would give way, which was verified some time after. The Captain knew nothing of the occurrence, and the remembrance of it was well-nigh obliterated, until in an unlucky hour the mounted sergeant, who knew nothing of what had occurred to the sword, was exhibiting it to some acquaintances, when in bending it into a hoop it snapped at the weld. In his consternation he hastily dropped the point half back into the scabbard, thrust the other in after it, and made a precipitate exit from the house without the servants suspecting what had occurred. Thus the sword remained for several weeks until its discovery by the Captain, the particulars of which must form the materials for a third chapter.

CHAPTER III

STORY OF A SWORD—*(Continued)*.

" Alas ! what perils do environ
The man that meddles with cold iron."
—HUDIBRAS.

AN Assizes is a big event in the capital of a county—the
county parliament as it were, big with anxious interest—a
species of general judgment-day, when every official has to
render an account of his stewardship, from the sub-inspector
down to the sub-constables who have cases on hand, from
the senior counsel to the solicitor, unravelling his knotty and
tangled web of evidence and testimony. The county-inspector of the R. I. C., furnishing his return of crime and
outrage, is anxious that no remark adverse to the state of his
county shall be heard from his lordship ; county-surveyors,
road-contractors, clerks of the peace, grand and petty
jurymen bustling about ; the court-keeper's fate hangs on
the state of the Court and the comfort of their lordships ;
witnesses in mortal dread of the cross-examination, heckling,
and roasting in store for them by opposite counsel ; and
lastly, the various prisoners awaiting trial, perhaps for a
lengthened period, racked with doubts and fears as to their
impending fate—

" The critch-owl, scrithing loud,
Puts the wretch that lies in woe
In remembrance of a shroud ".

Sub-Inspector D—— of Parsonstown was the officer
detailed for Court duty during the Assizes held at the capital
of the King's County. To the uninitiated I have to explain
that one of the functions of an officer told off for this duty

is to receive the judges on their arrival with all the available police, the ceremony consisting of a general salute, "present arms," which, as I have already explained, necessitates the drawing of the officer's sword. Now the Captain, being a military man, was usually selected for such duties, for no man could rival him when military exercises were to be gone through. " I'd make my men," he would say, " wheel on a plate." On the day in question the judges duly arrived, and the Captain, at the head of a large party of police, drawn up contiguous to where their lordships were to alight from their carriage. He had on his precious " Toledo," as was his wont on State occasions, but he little suspected the disaster which the inside of the scabbard could reveal. This was the first occasion since it was broken that he had used it. Presently their lordships' carriage was seen approaching, and just as it stopped where they were to alight, the Captain, with a last caution to his men to " wait for the last sound of the word and do it as one man," drew forth, with the usual clang and flourish, the " Toledo," when, horror of horrors ! he holds not his beautiful blade in its entirety, but a stump of its former self ! His figure was ludicrous in the extreme, and a titter ran through the crowd of people looking on ; some wag said audibly, " Is that a bacon knife the Captain has ? " Now the dreadful discovery he made of his treasured weapon being broken swallowed and absorbed every other earthly consideration around and about him ; time, place, circumstance, presence were alike obliterated in that one fatal glance at the mutilated sword. The judges of the land dwindled into insignificance when his great calamity was fully realised, and instead of giving the order " Present arms," their lordships were received with what they conceived was a volley of anathemas, epithets, threats, and abuse directed at them, much to their amazement and mystification. When the Captain realised the fact that it was really his " Toledo " that was broken, he rushed out in front of the men, and in his rage shouted out, " Scoundrels, villains, rogues, thieves, robbers, murderers, which of you broke my sword ? Oh, death and daggers ! I'll make a corpse of someone ! Fire and bombshells ! can anyone tell me who broke my sword? By high Olympus, I'll dismiss every man of you from my district of Parsonstown if I find out you know who has done it and you refuse to reveal his name! If it has been done here in Tullamore since I came, I warrant you I'll find it out." The Captain's frame of mind regarding these two towns at that moment was exactly the same as that of the poet who wrote in his ire—

> "Great Bog of Allen, swallow down
> That odious heap called Phillipstown (Parsonstown),
> And if thy maw can swallow more,
> Pray take (and welcome) Tullamore".

In the middle of his wrath a vague suspicion shot across him that "Big John," who was at the right of the line of men, had a hand in it, from the fact that he had caught him one day exhibiting the sword to friends. Rushing at him he yelled, "Oh, you huge brute, I could almost swear it was you who did it; but, by Jupiter, if I can find it out I'll——" and he shook the giant in the ranks, at which that placid individual put on a grin at the pigmy who held him, which tended to add fuel to the fire of his superior officer's wrath.

Now as I said their lordships were startled at the novel reception they received in Tullamore on their arrival; it was something so different from the usual way the "majesty of the law" was wont to be treated that they both paused to observe the cause. It so happened that both were thorough humourists of the type of the old school; and after taking in the scene, they thoroughly enjoyed it, and bandied from one to the other a running fire of facetious remarks by way of commentary on the sub-inspector's strange conduct.

"What really is the matter with this strange person?" said one.

"Don't you perceive," replied the other, "someone has broken his sword. See the stump of it in his hand. I see it all at a glance."

"Yes, I see it, and he is shaking it at that large constable. David and Goliath."

" 'What's but a choleric word in the captain is rank blasphemy in the soldier.' Shakespeare to wit."

"That's good I admit, but this more apposite, ' 'Tis thus the *half-sword* parleying Romans spake'. Epitaph on Shakespeare to wit."

" Yes, that *is* good, I admit ; but do you think did Ajax defy the lightning this way ?"

At this juncture the county-inspector, a most prosaic and matter-of-fact sort of man, who saw from a distance that something was wrong, came on the scene, and, running up to the Captain, gasped out—

"What ! what's the matter ? Good heavens, man, what are you about, or what has happened ?"

"The matter !" vociferously exclaimed the Captain ; "here's what's the matter. Look at my precious weapon broken by some miscreant !"

"And is it for that you raise such a hubbub ? Such nonsense ! all about an old sword. Trash, man ! I wonder at you. What'll their lordships say at such unseemly conduct on your part ?"

Now this was not throwing oil on the troubled waters, and the Captain, losing all control of himself, yelled out—

"All about an old sword, forsooth ! Do you know what it is ? I think more of that sword than the whole lock-stock-and-barrel of your law-sharks put together. It has been in places where one of them dare not show his face."

" Good gracious, man !" exclaimed the "County," raising his hands in a deprecatory manner, "have you lost your senses ? Get the men into Court at once. Right turn, men, quick march ; take your places in Court," and away bustled the " County" and left the irate Captain to himself, and so ended this portion of the little drama of the sword.

When the Assizes were over the Captain held a kind of star-chamber inquiry touching the mishap, and elicited that " Big John " was the delinquent. A terrific scene took place when they met, and the Captain intimated that he would report the matter to the inspector-general. However, " Big John " craved a respite, until he took the weapon

up to Lord Rosse again. When the latter saw it he said,
" 'Tis as well ; I told you it wouldn't stand the strain. I'll
convince the Captain now that I can measure swords with
him ; I'll produce a *facsimile* of this blade, and show him—
and Toledo, ay, or Damascus either—that we can temper
in Ireland as nicely as they can."

In a week his lordship produced a blade, a perfect *facsimile* of the old one, in every device and particular, with
an equally elastic temper, much to the wonder and satisfaction of the Captain. He kept, of course, the old *souvenir*,
and prized it as much as ever. He used to pull out the
stump and facetiously inform visitors that the scabbard had
devoured the other half, which was just the reverse of what
happened to Hudibras, whose sword *ate half the scabbard :*—

> " The trenchant blade, Toledo trusty,
> For want of fighting was grown rusty,
> And ate itself for lack
> Of somebody to hew and hack.
> The peaceful scabbard where it dwelt
> The rancour of its edge had felt ;
> For of the lower end two handful
> It had devoured, 'twas so manful,
> And so much scorned to lurk in case,
> As if it durst not show its face."

I may add to this sketch that after the two judges
walked away some bystanders overheard them continuing
the badinage—

" ' Scoundrels, villains !' *et cætera.* Which of us, my lord,
has this person found out ?"

" ' Thieves, robbers !' *et cætera,*" parried the other ; " I may
remind your lordship *you* were the *first* out of the carriage,
consequently, the first he laid eyes on. There's no sophistry
about this man."

" ' By high Olympus, I'll make a corpse of somebody !'
He was looking in your lordship's direction at the particular
moment he uttered that terrific threat."

Just a few more incidents in the closing portion of the
career of the biggest man in the force. The last visit of

the Queen to Ireland was in 1861, on the occasion of the
Prince of Wales finishing his military training with the
Guards, then stationed on the Curragh. It was a red-letter
day also for the old Curragh, where Royal visits were like
those of angels, few and far between.   The Curragh had
not witnessed the presence of Royalty in the person of the
Sovereign since the memorable visit of George the Fourth
in 1821.   A brilliant and memorable "gathering of the
clans" was also the result, when the notabilities of the
Empire, civil and military, made the Curragh *pro tem.* the
nucleus of the United Kingdom, the Sovereign herself being
the central figure.   In this great assembly of people from
all parts of Ireland, some remarkable men were pointed out
to Her Majesty, among whom was "Big John" as a "particularly large man".   The Queen looked at him steadily
for some time, and, it is alleged, made this remark :—" I
remember that on the occasion of my first visit to Ireland
there was a very fine body of men of the Constabulary
marched by at the review in the Phœnix Park ".

After he had retired on pension, he was returning one
evening from the Curragh races to his home, when he was
set upon by a mob of pickpockets, thieves, and thimble-
riggers, who knew him and had a spite against him.   They
waylaid him in a lonesome part of the Curragh, and a terrific encounter took place ; although "Big John" was
fearfully outnumbered he dealt terrible havoc amongst
them.   I remember well that night.   Our officer, a young
cadet, called for two men to accompany him on patrol.   We
marched to the Curragh on account of the races, and as we
approached a dip or hollow we noticed a number of dark
bodies lying on the ground ; one was a very large one in
comparison to the others.   " What are those do you think ?"
asked the officer.   " I should say a horse and a number of
asses," replied my comrade, A——.   When we approached
them, A—— exclaimed, " No, no, sir ; they are men ".
" So they are," remarked the officer, and stooping down he
looked into the face of the large man, and exclaimed, " Good
heavens ! why, this is my late head-constable, and he seems
to be dead ! he has been murdered probably ! "   This re-

mark, along with the words "dead, murdered," seemed to
arouse "Big John" from his torpor, and we heard him
• mutter in his great deep voice, or rather grumble in his
Munster brogue—"Murdhered, dead ; not yet, although
very near it; I'm not kilt as yet; but how many *is* kilt?
Count them, there must be seven ; and after that count the
arms and legs that's broken, and the number of scalps that
you'll find on the ground. They attacked me, but they
rued it before it was all over. Murdhered indeed! d'ye
think it's so easy to murdher me?" Indeed the scene was
just a good unrehearsed one of that amusing passage in
"Henry the Fourth," where Prince Henry finds Falstaff
apparently dead on the battlefield :—

Prince Henry. "What, old acquaintance ! could not all this flesh
Keep in a little life? Poor Jack, farewell !
I could have better spared a better man.
O, I should have a heavy miss of thee,
If I were much in love with vanity.
Death hath not struck so fat a deer to-day,
Though many dearer, in this bloody fray
Embowelled will I see thee by-and-by :
Till then in blood by noble Percy lie"—*(Exit)*.

Falstaff (rising slowly). "Embowelled! If thou embowel me to-day, I
give you leave to powder me, and eat me to-morrow. S'blood, 'twas time to
counterfeit, or that hot tarmagent Scot had paid me scot and lot too.
Counterfeit? I lie; I am no counterfeit. To die is to be a counterfeit, for
he is but the counterfeit of a man, who hath not the life of a man ; but to
counterfeit dying when a man thereby liveth is to be no counterfeit. The
better part of valour is discretion," etc., etc.

We managed to get him on his legs, and it took us all
three to convey him towards the military hospital, where we
intended leaving him and then return and look after his
assailants. When we had got him halfway to that place, such
were the wonderful recuperative powers of the man's frame,
that he found himself little the worse of his beating, and
chose to proceed home to his house, where we left him,
and then proceeded to the scene of the fight, when not a
trace of the parties could be seen. I learned subsequently
that their "faking" friends had come in our absence and

taken the wounded parties away on their vehicles, and before our return they were well on their road to Dublin ; we heard no more of them.

The manner in which this remarkable man "shuffled off the mortal coil" was in keeping with his great physical powers, and the hallucination which was the cause of his tragic ending. The recklessness and daring which characterised him through life followed him to the close.   To supplement his pension, he got a situation in a distant part of Ireland, where *poteen* was of the purest spring, and that volatile liquor produced the delusion in his mind that he was a second Hercules. He had often read of that mythical personage's exploits, such as killing the Nemean lion, the Lernean hydra, the cleansing of the Augean stables, the strangling of the serpents, conquering the giants, etc., and in his frenzy he determined to emulate him.   He procured an enormous limb of an ash-tree, and flourishing it as a club, he proceeded to a railway track and said he would outdo Hercules in all his feats, by stopping the engine and train with one blow.   Taking his place on the middle of the track, he put a bottle of *poteen* to his mouth when the train came in sight, and, apostrophising the approaching engine, said, " Here's yer health and song, ma'am, an' if ye don't pull up I'll make smithereens of ye with my club, for I am Hercules the second," flourishing the limb of the ash-tree.   The engine-driver, leaning over the side of the engine, his face pale as a sheet and his eyes starting from their sockets with horror, gesticulated wildly to no use, while he let off the engine's loudest whistle and scream. A great thud was heard as Big John struck the front of the iron horse, and in an instant the mortal career of the biggest man in the service was ended.

ECCENTRIC UNITS.

"H. B."

Eccentric persons will crop up in all ranks and positions in society, and their eccentric doings will be always amusing to read of; but eccentricity in authority, such as in the army or navy or police, will be far more amusing than any other. The Royal Irish Constabulary has been prolific of much eccentricity, and the most amusing man coming under this category in the force was an officer whom I shall designate under the initials of " H. B.," the familiar sobriquet by which he was known in the force. I remember him well, an under-sized, squat, thick-set man, lithe and active notwithstanding ; a rubicund visage like the full moon in a fog, shaved to a miracle. He was generally dressed in a shabby, threadbare suit of plain clothes, albeit the richest officer in the force ; and when he donned uniform an antiquated outfit of about the period of the first formation of the force was all he thought necessary. As conservative in his views and instincts as a Chinese mandarin, he viewed every innovation, in the shape of new patterns of uniform and equipments, with the most rabid and ineradicable hostility. To give a practical proof of this hatred of reform, he doggedly refused to purchase one iota of new regulation uniform or outfit, and always wore on duty the old paraphernalia he rejoiced in some thirty years before, braving, with the philosophy of a Stoic, the ridicule it brought on him when he appeared therein at Assizes, elections, petty sessions, etc. Shaving was with him, as like most of the old school, a species of religious rite, a mania, and the unlucky wight caught, or even suspected of, not applying the razor to his chin each morning was looked upon as a delinquent of the worst type. *En passant*, it may be remarked that this rage for a clean-shaved visage was not an oddity confined to " H. B." Shaving in the old times, under the iron *régime* of the Duke of Wellington, was a " rite " so orthodox that, in a disciplinary sense, nothing could save the soldier from condign punishment who was caught *in flagrante delicto* with the incipient stubble of a night's growth on his chin. It will perhaps be remembered by a good many how Dr. Russell, the *Times* special correspondent in the Crimea, thundered against the outrageous martinetism of General Sir George Brown, compelling the soldiers to shave every morning, and how with razors that became like reaping-hooks the unfortunate " Tommy Atkinses " appeared as if the enemy were amusing themselves over night with the points of their swords at their chins and jaws. When the order of Colonel John Stewart Wood, allowing the men of the force to wear beards, was issued, it almost set "H. B." out of his mind. He threatened and fumed and shook his clenched fist at any man who had the hardihood to take advantage of the privilege. Despotic as a Turkish Bashaw, he ruled his district with an iron hand ; and the couplet illustrating his peculiar mode of governing, and his eccentric despotism, might be quoted to give an idea of his quality—

> " All hail, all hail to the great Bashaw ;
> His frown is death and his word is law ".

Yet, beneath all his eccentric despotism, he meant well for the men under him, and many men who could never save a penny anywhere else became comparatively prosperous and well-to-do when they came to serve in his district. Thrifty and provident himself, he compelled all under him to follow his example ; and for this purpose he instituted a code of bye-laws, one of which was that every man under his command should have an account in the savings bank, and should produce the book containing it at each monthly inspection, where it was duly scrutinised and examined. Woe betide the individual whose improvident and spend-thrift habits precluded the possibility of an account to his credit, and unremitting woe likewise awaited the individual who could not give a satisfactory account of his expenditure during the month, or the why or wherefore the usual deposit was not made and entered in the book.

" Well, O'Halloran, how comes it you haven't made your usual deposit after last month's pay, and I perceive you've withdrawn to a considerable amount ? "

" I couldn't put in any, sir, and was obleeged to take out ten pound."

" What's become of the money? Give me a strict account."

" It's in the landlord's pocket by this time, sir ; my father asked me to send him what would pay the last gale of rent, and sure, sir, I could not stand by and see the ould place gone from the family."

" Humph ; if it's gone that way it is well; but take care it isn't the landlord of the public-house has got it."

" Oh, no, sir ; I can show ye my father's letter."

" It is well for your father and yourself you've come to my district ; you had just three halfpence on your arrival, now you've got one hundred pounds to your account."

" Well, O'Flagherty, what have you to say as to the why and wherefore your last month's deposit is not entered here ? "

" I had to buy a pair of boots, sir."

" A pair of boots wouldn't cost two pounds, would they ? You had better mind what you're at, and drop your old spendthrift ways in my district. Do you remember, sir, when you came to me, and on my first inspection of you I found on examination of your box of necessaries one plain clothes coat of so fragile a texture and old that the moths had long since given it up as not worth making a meal on, and when I took it into my hand it fell into fragments beneath my touch, literally dissolved, and collapsed like a cobweb; you had a structure you called trousers which should be set down as in the singular number, for it had only one leg, as if it had belonged to a man with a wooden leg ; and when I demanded an explanation as to why your trousers had only one leg, you laid the blame on a dog and the moths, conjointly ; you had a towel rolled up and pretended it was a shirt; you were somewhat of an improvement on Sir John Falstaff, who had only one shirt in his whole company of recruits, and that was a towel ; you had a thing you called a waistcoat made of brown paper and dyed with a solution of boiled logwood and copperas ; you had a hat which a scarecrow might envy, and every necessary you had was in keeping with those ; you had the articles mentioned supported by a structure of wooden uprights in your box to pretend it was packed full and solid, but such devices cannot be palmed off on me. I made you another man ; you've an account at your bankers ; valuable clothes and necessaries fill your box ; don't degenerate into your old improvident, spendthrift ways. I hope I'll see this rectified on my next inspection; *you* ought to dread folly and

5

squandering, for I knew your family and what it brought them down to."

And thus Rhadamanthus-like he compelled every man to give a strict account of his "stewardship" each month as to the way the money was expended, and ingenious and ludicrous were the pleas and excuses devised to answer his scrutiny.

His manner of inspecting his stations and his peculiar mode of enforcing discipline were in keeping with all his other eccentric ways. Despotic, as I have already said, as an oriental potentate, whose reputed method of governing was by the scimitar or bastinado, or, emulating the hero of one of Lever's racy lyrics, the inimitable "Larry M'Hale," who—

" With a cruel four-pounder kept all in great order,
But his favourite weapon was always a flail ".

" H. B." ruled with an enormous blackthorn cudgel, a sharp penknife, and a scissors. The two latter instruments were for cutting, trimming, and pruning everything which, according to *his* views, was not *per* regulation, such as ends of straps, tufts of hair, curls, fringes, whiskers, moustachios, etc., so that the ground, after an inspection, appeared as if a gardener had been pruning a row of fruit-trees. When the inspection was over it was a ludicrous sight to witness each man contemplating the amount of damage he had sustained. Here were a couple of Adonises *minus* their ambrosial curls or dainty "fringes," others lamenting over mutilated straps, whose ends lay with another man's *whisker* on the parade ground, while the owner of the hirsute appendage was ruefully surveying his appearance in the mirror with its fellow still intact. But a station escaped with comparative safety if it was confined to the "pruning" process referred to ; when the barrack windows, plain clothes, delf, and furniture were not smashed, torn, and injured, the sergeant and his party might consider themselves lucky.

Like Larry M'Hale, who kept all in great order by a process peculiarly his own, so did " H. B.," by a summary jurisdiction quite his own, and never contemplated by the rules and regulations of the service, preserve order amongst his subjects, the police. It is a well-known circumstance that where a district is disorderly, *i.e.*, among the police themselves, where turbulence takes the place of peace, and reports reach headquarters, the officer in charge feels that a certain portion of the disrepute attaches to himself, inasmuch as the head authorities consider that if he exercised proper control and supervision, such a state of things could not exist. It is therefore the interest of all officers to have few reports for indiscipline. It is also a well-known phase of the force that when an officer gets a "knuckling" from headquarters, he, by way of reprisals, knuckles his district or the particular station or stations that were the cause of it. This generally takes the shape of great exactness on inspection, frequent visits by night and by day, reports of the slightest infraction of the regulations and discipline, extra or "revenge duty" ordered, etc., etc. How did "H. B." visit his delinquent stations? He despised these conventional devices just mentioned as mean and puerile; he came at the pockets of the party of men in his erring stations by a process, as I've said, peculiarly his own. He considered that by adopting the *rôle* of the rigid disciplinarian, by way of reprisals, and patiently waiting until he could get, or manufacture, a report against the sergeant or his men, he would be simply giving himself trouble and annoyance. If a fine was inflicted on one man from headquarters *he* made sure that the rest of the party participated in the pecuniary loss of the delinquent. Like our friend Larry M'Hale, whose favourite weapon was a flail, "H. B." made use of the enormous blackthorn stick mentioned, with which he smashed the barrack windows, the mess delf, the furniture, or any "breakable" utensil that he saw or could lay hands on, and then "leathered" away at the backs of the erring ones. However, he was just in his mode of reprisals on a station, for he meted out, on a very fair scale, the amount of *damage* to the *gravity* of the offence. For instance, for one case of intoxication he smashed all the windows; for two, occurring within a certain period, he smashed all the mess delf, in addition to the windows; for three, he added the destruction of the furniture and utensils,

and in aggravated cases he flung the station bedding and
books out through the wrecked windows as a grand *finale* to
his other exploits.   If the odium of an "investigation into
charges, etc.," fell on him in any station, he tore into
"flibbans" all the plain or private clothes in the station.
Now this high-handed method of keeping "all in great order"
had more efficacy and virtue in it all than all the terrors of
the code of regulations, for inasmuch as the delinquency of
one or two individuals brought condign punishment on every
man, it was incumbent on all alike to restrain and check the
turbulent and erring ones.   Of course the repairs of the
wrecked station, the replacing of the delf, utensils, plain
clothes, etc., fell on the whole party alike.   As the straw
shows how the wind blows, so did the men of his own or
headquarter station observe that a storm was brewing and
was ready to burst over the heads of some unlucky party in a
station of his district, when H. B. brought forth from its
resting-place over his kitchen fireplace, where it lay "season-
ing" in peaceful times, the enormous blackthorn.   This
cudgel, or rather alpeen, he would carry about with him for
a few days before he made the foray, probably to accustom
and "train" his hand in for the anticipated raid, and the
remarks regarding this "preliminary" were significant:—
    "Eh, what! begor, did ye see 'H. B.' with the 'black-
thorn'?   What barrack is he goin' to wrack, Tom, d'ye
know?"
    "Oh, didn't ye hear of the holy murdher in Ballyhooly
station?   Sure, Sargint Hagerty reported Oulahan for bein'
dhrunk comin' home from the fair of Ballyknockdholdrum,
and didn't Doolan and Muloughney fight about Mary
Muldoon—a girl o' the Muldoons of Branish—and all is
reported?"
    "Oh, good jewel, d'ye say so, Tom?   Oh, by the piper of
Blessinton, he'll not lave a whole pane o' glass in the barrack,
an' I wish the delf luck; an' sure maybe he'll reef the clothes,
an' Heally bought a new suit, an' there'll be the fun."
    Then it was amusing to observe the alarm of some old
staid, anxious sergeant, from whose station a report or two
had gone in.

" Oh, murdher, murdher, what'll I do at all? Oh, ye vagabones, if yez don't conduct yerselves he'll come out an' wrack me ; an' it's not me but yerselves'll suffer as well."

It was a singular sight to witness the scene after his departure from a wrecked barrack. Here was the sergeant ruefully surveying the fractured glass and its extent ; there a " sub " contemplating a tremendous rent in his coat, waistcoat, or inexpressibles ; the cook lamenting over the ruins of her delf—bowls, plates, dishes, cups, saucers, etc.—all in " one red burial blent".

" Oh, look at me chaynee ! look at me chaynee ! all made smithereens of be that divil of a man."

Now probably the curious reader may ask how could any man carry on so high-handed a line of procedure and escape the consequences. " H. B." did higher-handed acts than those detailed, for he drove a " coach-and-four " through the rules and regulations by instituting himself as county-inspector in a county he had served in as sub-inspector. In addition to this he established his headquarters in a remote village in the *ultima thule* or farthest corner of the county, ignoring the three or four chief towns, snapped his fingers in the face of the grand jury, and remained there in spite of them. In comparison to this feat such a trifle as his " Larry M'Hale " work was only child's play. Supposing that some crusty litigant reported him for the damage done to his property, " H. B." made good the amount forthwith ; but that same individual invariably rued the hour in which he put pen to paper on the matter. By repute the richest officer in the service, he could afford to run the risk of playing the despot. All refractory and incorrigible men were sent to his district as a species of reformatory ; and they knew they had only two alternatives under him—to behave themselves or to retire from the force. " I'll send you to Mr. ——'s district," the county-inspector used to say to defaulters, and in many cases this threat had the desired effect, for the wholesome dread of such a contingency always hung like the sword of Damocles over the heads of the erring ones.

When he appeared on duty at Assizes, races, fairs, etc., his

appearance caused a good deal of remark by those who did
not know him. Attired in a uniform of a bygone time,
threadbare and seedy, a Falstaffian figure from which issued
a voice deep-pitched and sonorous, he was the cynosure of
all eyes, and his *outré tout ensemble* was a source of infinite
amusement to many young officers. Their remarks might
be summed up thus :

"Oh ! by Jove, Harry, look here ! What apparition is
this ?   An animated barrel or the ghost of Sir John
Falstaff ! "

Harry adjusts his eyeglass to have a look at the "apparition," which very shortly asserts its corporeal quality of a
substance that can make itself felt by other flesh and blood.
As it is already shown, " H. B." was a despot of the first water ;
he thought as little of his juniors when he was sub-inspector,
and of his officers when he was promoted county-inspector,
as of the humblest sub-constable ; and when the titter ran
among the young officers on his first appearance, he in very
short time made them "laugh at the wrong sides of their
mouths," to use a familiar saying.   He probably felt that he
was a butt for laughter, and he balanced the scale by wheel-
ing those into line who came under his thumb. For instance,
on the parade ground at an Assizes or races, etc., Messrs.
Sub-Inspectors Harry, Dick, and Robert are seen curiously
scanning the senior Sub-Inspector " H. B.," who is approaching the assembled group. It is the first time they
have seen him, and his grotesque appearance and ancient
uniform supplies food for much mirth at his expense. A
grin mantles on each countenance which, in a very short
time, is reversed from *l'allegro* to *il penseroso*. With a quick
glance at the group " H. B." takes in every man's shortcomings. One or two have their forage caps on when they
should have their shakos ; another is in his undress frock
when he should be in his tunic ; another is *minus* his sword ;
and so on. Pausing a moment, like a lion calculating his
spring on his prey, with knitted brows, " H. B." fiercely
surveys the group, and at length in a voice of thunder he
opens fire on them :—

"How comes it that you two are not properly dressed ?

Where's your shakos? Is this the manner you mean to do duty here? Away, sirs, this instant, and appear in your shakos. How is it that you haven't your tunic on? Away, sir, and I'll give you five minutes to be back here again for parade. What is this for? What's become of your sword? Get away, sir, and appear here properly equipped; five minutes, or mark the consequences." Then to the remaining individuals who are "point device" in their dress, " Close your heels, sirs, and stand to attention!"

There was one peculiarity about him, and, *en passant*, it is a remarkable and well-known idiosyncrasy not confined to the eccentric " H. B.," *i.e., don't look at him.* With him and a number of other officers it was an unpardonable offence to watch, look, or stare at them. Like the "veiled Prophet of Khorassan," it was death to those who were unlucky enough to have seen his face, so, woe betide the man found gratifying his curiosity by scanning his officer's face or figure. "Look to your front, sir," he thunders at the delinquent, "and don't be watching me. You'll have enough to do to watch yourself."

With such a man it is natural to suppose that a frequent change of servants should take place. In those times it was the rule to allow officers to select a man from the rank-and-file to act as major-domo, footman, coachman, butler, etc., all rolled into one; and as there was usually a sprinkling of men whose avocation before joining lay in this direction, there was no great difficulty in procuring men suited for such a post. From his eccentric ways and despotic disposition, " H. B's." orderlies were frequently exchanged; and as he could not always procure a man suited to such functions, he had to put up with raw, untrained men, or some unsophisticated awkward youth whose only qualification was holding the handles of his father's plough before joining. Like all people aspiring to be thought fashionable and who are not yet beyond that rubicon which bounds the region of the *crème-de-la-crème*, " H. B." was anxious and emulous of cutting a respectable figure when out driving, so that he bestowed great care on the appearance and cut of his vehicle, horses, harness, servant, and so forth. Now when a new man

of the category just mentioned took up the post, it was a
sight for gods and men to see him being trained to his
functions by the eccentric officer.   To any one who could
with privacy and safety view from a distance this training-in,
it was provocative of unrestrained mirth, but to those engaged
in it, namely, the new orderly himself and two or three
cavalry policemen, it was quite the reverse.   At one period
of his service " H. B." was stationed in a district near Dublin, where he frequently drove to for shopping purposes, so
that he was sensitive and keenly alive to the *éclat* of cutting,
not alone a respectable, but an aristocratic figure in the capital,
so that no one should scoff, sneer, or " snuff " at his outfit.
For this object his new orderly underwent a course of training
for several days, in the following manner.   He selected his
coach-yard as the training, or rather rehearsal ground, and
it was supposed to be the city, the out offices, the 'leading
establishments in which shopping was to be done or business
transacted.   The coach-house was " M'Swiney's and Dela-
ney's," the gate having the name chalked thereon; the stable
was " Todd's and Burns'," the harness-room " MacBirney's,"
and so on with the " General Post-office," " Custom House,"
" Bank of Ireland," etc.   He then caused his phaeton to be
brought out, and two cavalry men were told off to get into
the shafts and act as horses, the neophyte taking his place
in the " dickey," whilst " H. B." himself presided on the front
seat.   The " horses " were told to " gee up," and away they
went dragging the vehicle and its occupants round and round
about the yard, stopping for " shopping purposes " at Todd's
and Burns' " or " MacSwiney's," etc., whilst the novice was
supposed to alight from the " dickey " gracefully and with
agility, dart into the establishment and deliver his orders
or perform his various functions on such occasions.   Now
this singular spectacle of two uniformed men in the shafts
of a phaeton, dragging two other persons round about the
premises and stopping at gates and doorways, whilst one
individual precipitately alighted and disappeared in through
the gate or doorway, forthwith made his appearance again,
and as speedily jumped up, sometimes stumbling and fall-
ing, at others barking his shins against the step by missing

it, while the other individual sat watching his movements, would be a source of much mystery to one who viewed it from a distance. "Now then," "H. B." would say, his rubicund visage purple with anger and disappointment at some particularly awkward recruit, "gee up, horses, quicken your pace, and when you come to it, stop at 'Todd's and Burns',' and let me see *you, fellow,* do it better this time. Fold yours arms, sir, and sit erect; don't think it's the plough you've a hold of now. Wo, horses. Oh, look at that! there's a clodhopper jumping down off the side of a dùng-cart. You'll never be anything but a lubber. Gee up, horses, and stop at MacBirney's, and *you,* fellow, go in and tell the attendants I want them, and don't go in with a mouth on you as if it was a fourpenny loaf you were going to buy. Wo, horses. Oh, there you are again; one would think with the big long steps you took it was a dish of stirabout you were making for, to be in time for your share."

Now to the rest of the party in the headquarters' station this process of training a new recruit was the climax of all fun if they could view it with safety; but woe betide the luckless wight caught peeping. There was only one safe place where it might be seen with a chance of escape, if detected. It was a wicket door in the boundary wall, shutting the premises off from the road, so that a good fleet runner could round the corner and reach the barrack before " H. B." could catch sight of him; and at this door, as if glued to it, with noses flattened against the door, and right or left eye opposite a chink or knot-hole admitting a view through, would be seen four or five men in uniform, like little boys at a peep-show, with two or three more waiting their turn. Some have their handkerchiefs thrust into their mouths to smother their laughter, and at length some individual, whose risible attribute is past all control, bursts into a loud "guffaw" as he sees the mounted Adonis of the station come along, trotting and sweating in the shafts of the phaeton, with " H. B.," like a Roman conqueror who compelled his captives to draw him in triumph into Rome, urging them to quicken their pace.

"Come, horses, stir yourselves; gee up; you're getting

lazy." The loud laugh at the wicket door is detected by
" H. B.," and suspecting its cause he makes a dash from the
phaeton, and in an instant his hand is on the key, and the
door is flung open just in time to get a glance at six or
seven pairs of heels carrying their owners round the corner
at top speed. Swift as a swallow, he is after them into the
barrack; but when there he finds no indication of any man
having been engaged in a race for life. Some are reading,
some writing, and all are calm and innocent looking. He
glares ferociously into each man's face. " I think it was
you, and you, and you, and if I could prove it I'd make you
suffer." " Oh," would be the " injured innocence " reply.
" Is it me, sir? Is it me, sir?" " If I could catch the
man or men," he'd thunder, "that have dared to come
prying into my premises, I'd make it a costly curiosity for
him."

There was one other singularity about him; it was a
deep-rooted antipathy to all sorts of fowls, chiefly arising
from the noises they produced, which seemed to give him
torture. The crowing of cocks, cackling of hens, quacking
of ducks, cawing of rooks and daws, and particularly the
din produced by small birds—sparrows, linnets, etc.—was to
him the same source of mental torture as the organ grinder
to the city, literary, or office man. Woe, unremitting woe,
awaited the village-duty sub-constable who allowed this
nuisance to exist, or, in like manner, allowed children to
play in the street, their boisterous laughter having a similar
effect on " H. B.'s " sensitive tympanum. The French
women after Waterloo used to frighten and hush their
troublesome children to rest with the name of the Duke
of Wellington in a nursery rhyme—

> " Baby, baby, he's a giant,
> Tall and as black as Rouen Steeple ".

So it was with the mothers in " H. B.'s " headquarters
town; the name of " H. B." was sufficient to still the most
obstreperous of children. The chief duty of the street duty-
man was to abate all these nuisances; and the curious
reader may query how could he have control over crows,

jackdaws, sparrows, hens, ducks, etc. There was no excuse for the duty-man when a system was laid down for him, and a weapon or implement provided, consisting of an enormously long pole, tapering away to the top like a fishing-rod, at the end of which was firmly attached a great bunch of long leather thongs like a cat-o'-nine-tails. With this instrument the man on duty was to pursue the recalcitrant crow, jackdaw, or sparrow. For this purpose he had frequently to visit " H. B.'s " premises and beat away at the trees, hedgerows, eaves, chimneys, etc., and then away through the fields after them, in " hunting the wren " style, to show how effectually and assiduously he was " performing his duty ". Sometimes an over-zealous man would remain away somewhat longer than the circumstance would require, but when questioned as to his absence he was very plausible and profuse in describing his zeal and all the trouble he had in the pursuit ; how he " followed the vagabones of crows all the way to the rookery," etc., etc. There was one young policeman who, when sent to be stationed in " H. B.'s " headquarters, adopted a line of action which he thought would be the safest to pull him through the difficulties and risks of serving in such a place. He pretended to be a simple unsophisticated youth, unversed in the devious paths of craft or cunning. He could only obey the orders he received, to the letter and literally, and perform his duty with zeal and alacrity.

" I'll always obay mee ordhers an' do what I'm towld," he would say, " for it's the first duty of a sodger, or polisman either, to do so, and I'll just do like the Rooshian sentry that let the wather up to his chin, an' then nobody can say anything to me."

Tom O'Flagherty, in emulating the sentry, made an attempt to find the *locale* of a certain place that shall be nameless, in obedience to his officer's orders. Shakespeare speaks of people who "travel the primrose path to the everlasting bonfire ". Tom didn't travel this primrose path, but, according to his own showing, a very thorny one, in his search for the said bonfire.

One May morning " H. B." rushed over to the barrack

with his fingers thrust into his tortured ears and called for the street duty-man, who proved to be Tom.

" How comes it, sir," thundered the irate officer at Tom, "that you're not doing your duty? Here I am tortured by those villainous birds and cannot perform my clerical work, and there you are, a great hulking worthless lubber. Go along, sir, and get the pole and rid me of them, and if you are not more on the alert to do your duty I'll have you fined."

"Arrah begor, plaze yer honour, sir, sure I'm doin' mee best, an' ain't I dhrivin' the vagabones away all day, an' sure they're coming back agin," pleaded Tom.

" Well, drive them away now," roared " H. B."

" Where'll I dhrive them them to, sir ? " asked Tom.

"Ah, go, sir, and give no lip; only drive them to h—ll out of this. Away, sir, and don't stand gaping at me, and do your duty."

" Yes, sir," replied Tom.

Away he went with alacrity and procured the bird pole from its resting-place along the wall, and laboured very industriously, beating away at the trees, hedgerows, eaves of houses, and the premises generally around his officer's house. After apparently ridding the precincts of the house of all the birds, fowls, and the like, he was observed very industriously following up his work along the high road in the direction of Dublin, apparently labouring very hard, shouting, hallooing, and " hushing " like a person driving a flock of sheep before him. However, to the uninitiated observer Tom's movements were somewhat inexplicable, inasmuch as the objects of his pursuit were nowhere to be seen. Probably Tom O'Flagherty was familiar with the belief of the poet Burns, who, touching the temporary residence of his satanic majesty, says—

" But this that I am gaun to tell,
Which lately on a night befell,
Is just as true as the deil's in hell,
    Or Dublin City."

For, in " obaydience to his ordhers," as he said, he drove his flock of birds to that city. The shades of evening had heralded the sombre pall of night, and with it tea-hour came, but Tom O'Flagherty was not in his place at the table; he had not been missed at dinner-hour, but his absence from the tea-table caused some surprise.

"Why is this fellow not here to his tea?" queried the sergeant. "I don't know," remarked the barrack-orderly, to whom the question was directed; "he wasn't in to his dinner either." "How is this?" said the sergeant. "I was at my monthly returns all day and hadn't time to look after him." So he put on his belt and sallied forth to search for Tom, having a strong misgiving that he would find the said Tom in some public house "under the influence". He diligently searched all the "pubs.," but there was no tidings of Tom in these bacchanalian retreats, and the sergeant returned much mystified as to his disappearance. Roll-call came at 10 o'clock p.m. but he was still *non est inventus*, and the "morn in russet mantle clad walked o'er the dew of the high eastern hills," but Tom O'Flagherty didn't walk over the hills with it to his barrack. Another day and night turned on their golden round, but heralded not the return of the missing sub-constable. Great alarm now pervaded the authorities as to what *could* have become of O'Flagherty, and diligent search and extensive inquiries were prosecuted in all directions as to his whereabouts, but his fate seemed wrapped in a cloud of mystery. Men were employed scouring the neighbourhood in every direction, but to no purpose. Dead or alive the lineal descendent of that recalcitrant Milesian clan, whose neighbours ejaculated in their daily orisons for protection—"From the ferocious O'Flaghertys, Lord, deliver us!"—was nowhere to be found. At length, on the evening of the third day, he presented himself suddenly before his officer, the bird-pole in his hand, seemingly much fatigued, and rubbing the sweat off his forehead with a threepenny handkerchief.

"Well, begor, sir," he broke out as he approached "H.B.," "that was a terrible job you gev me to do. Sorra so tough a job I ever got in my life, barrin' one time before I joined. Mee father sint me to the pound ten miles away wid oul' Lanty Hoolahan's four heifers an' three racers of pigs that.

trespassed on our oats, an' a hard job I had of them sure enough, but thim vagabones of birds bate them hollow."

"What are you talking about, sir, and where have you been for the last three days?" sternly demanded "H. B."

"Where have I been?" repeated Tom wonderingly. "Arrah now, yer jokin', sir; sure, wasn't I where ye sent me."

"Where did I send you, sir? How come you to be absent without leave for three days, and also deserting your post on town duty? This will dismiss you now," thundered "H. B."

"Oh, mother o' Moses, listen to this now," yelped Tom, putting on a look of injured innocence and oppressed virtue. " Didn't ye tell me, sir, to dhrive the vagabones of crows, jackdaws, and sparrows to h—ll, and when you abused me for not doin' mee duty, mee dandher was up, and I said I'd be abused no more, so I gother a great flock of them vaga- bone birds an', in fact, everything I met in the shape of fowl. I didn't even spare Jack Doolan's lame duck, that makes more noise than any of them. An' I said if the ould boy was fond ov crow's mate I'd give him lots to roast ; so I dhruv them afore me in a great flock towards Dublin. But, begor, it put me to the pin o' mee collar to keep them together, for they gave me grate throuble intirely ; Lanty Hoolahan's bastes wor far easier to manage. Well, I axed people as I went along where might I find h—ll, and they towld me it wasn't far from me, and if I could get into the place they call the Liberty I wouldn't be far from it by any manes, so I endayvoured to make mee way to the Liberty ; but, me jewel an' darlint sir, when I got into the city the flamin' rogues of birds bothered mee intirely to keep them together, an' I had to purshoo them up one street and down another, an' all the gossoons runnin' after me shoutin' out— ' Oh, here's a mad polisman from the country '. They thought I was mad. Well, yer honour, sure whin I seen thim scatterin' in all directions I got so mad that I made a divil of a welt at one vagabone of a crow that gave me more trouble than all the birds put together, as he was makin' away over a chimbley, whin, sir, the tails of the pole cotch in the

chimbleys, and down comes all the bricks tumblin' an'
tatherin' about mee ears. Musha, bad win' to them ould
Dublin chimbleys; there's not a bit of morthar keepin' thim
together. Well thin, out runs the people and cotch a howlt
o' me for the price o' the chimbley, so I had no money
about me an' I had to write home to mee freinds for it;
so this mornin' I got an ordher for the money from me
father, and here I am back again as quick as I could, an'
sure it's cowld comfort I'm gettin' for doin' what I was bid."

Now this ludicrous and barefaced narrative was delibe-
rately spoken by Tom looking into his officer's face without
a muscle moving, but with the expression of an ill-used
person, whilst the irascible officer looked as if he'd annihi-
late Tom.

There was one thing "H. B." dreaded, and that was an
exposure of his eccentricities, so that Tom, who was an
astute person in his way, knew how to frame a story that
would stave off the consequences of his escapade. He
simply took three days' leave for his amusement in Dublin,
and when he got a bit away from the village he hid the
bird-pole outside a hedge, from whence he fetched it on his
way back.

"Go along, you scheming, lying vagabond," growled
"H. B.," "to your duty; you're more rogue than fool.
Don't think you'll trifle with me. To your duty, sir, and
be sure if you're at this work again you'll not get off so
easy."

"Yes, sir," said Tom; "but will you allow the money
the oul' rotten chimbley cost me?"

"Away, sir; out of my sight with you!" roared the now
enraged "H. B.," and Tom beat a retreat to his barrack,
chuckling over his escape from a serious charge.

It was obvious that Tom, if reported for his absence,
would make a defence, setting forth the circumstance of the
"ordher he recaved," which was the very thing "H. B."
did not want the head authorities to know anything about.
The result was the immunity of many a man from the consequences of absence without leave, as well as the more
adventurous Tom.

Poor "H. B." is long since gone over to the majority,
and with all his fee-faw-fum ways he meant well for those
under him.   Thrifty and frugal himself, he compelled his
subordinates to go and do likewise.
I may mention that when the late Colonel Wood became
Inspector-General he sent an "ultimatum" to "H. B." to
"sell or sail," the meaning of which laconic order was
that "H. B." should take his county headquarters into the
chief town of the county from the remote village in which
he persisted remaining, or leave the service.   He chose the
latter alternative.

"TIGER TOWNSHEND."

Mr. Sub-Inspector Townshend was, by original profession,
instinct, and way of thinking, essentially a civilian.   He was
a well-known figure in the days of O'Connell's agitation.
Formerly editor and proprietor of a Cork Conservative paper,
he received the sobriquet of "Tiger" by the violence, almost
amounting to ferocity, of his leading articles on political subjects.   A fierce and forbidding expression of countenance
was also in keeping with the tone of his writings.   To use
the simile of a contemporary of his time, it was as if a "red
Indian were flourishing a tomahawk or scalping-knife in
every line".   Becoming bankrupt when the great depression
began to be felt in Ireland, Mr. Townshend's journal became
defunct; and having done yeoman's service for his party, the
Tories, they were bound in return to do something for him
when in office.   They therefore gave him a vacant sub-
inspectorship in the Constabulary.   As to putting him
through a preliminary course of drill and training, such was
eschewed altogether in his case, or he went through it as a
mere matter of form.   He scarcely knew the very rudiments
of that intricate science, and naturally cared less for knowing
it, from the very fact, as stated, that his profession and
instincts were essentially "civilian" before his appointment.
To use his own phrase on the matter, it was "like getting
a Delaware Indian to master the details of the Court of
Chancery as himself to master the mazes and intricacies of

drill ". However, he managed to smooth over his difficulty by an ingenious system of his own, when necessity compelled him to be in a position where drill movements were required. He had a set of words of command of his own coinage, which the men of his own district knew thoroughly, and they could interpret from them what he wished to be done as well, if not better, as the regular drill phraseology. At an election, Assizes, races, fair, etc., when the men should " fall in, double rank," he would give the following extraordinary order in a broad Cork accent, " Rare rank, turn yerselves inside out and then look to yer front ". Now this extraordinary order was quite rational after all, for the rear rank were looking inwards, and a right-about-face made them "turn themselves inside out," and form a new front for themselves. " March on a bit and dhrive that crowd before ye and stop when you come to the channel." Now the rear rank finding some difficulty in putting back the demonstrative mob, he orders the front rank to go to their assistance, and gives a similar word of command, except that instead of being told to " turn themselves inside out," it is " outside in ". " Front rank, turn yerselves outside in and go help the rare rank." He would sometimes tell a line of men to " turn their backs to the front and look to their rare ". New men coming to his district, on first hearing his singular orders, would be so mystified thereby that they would stand stock-still while the rest moved to the order.

" What's the matther with those two men ? Why don't ye move at the ordher? Didn't ye hear me give the ordher to turn yerselves inside out, or yer backs to yer front and look to yer rare ? "

" We don't undherstand the manin' of it, sir," they would reply. " We never was drilled that way before."

" Ye don't undherstand a simple ordher, simpler than any dhrill ye ever heard," he would say. " What childhre ye are ! D'ye know where your bellies are ? "

" Yes, sir, we do," was the answer.

" Well, d'ye know where yer backs are ? "

" Yes, sir, we do."

" Well, turn yer bellies where yer backs are and yer backs
where yer bellies are. Isn't that plain enough ? "

They make a right-about-face, and he exclaims, "Ay,
indeed, ye found it out at last ! "

Then he would order a party to "make a row by the
channel and dhress by the pump, and put yer bayonets on
yer guns ; and, head-constable, will you go along the row
and see if their powdher and ball is right and no rust on
their guns or irons ? "

Coupled with a forbidding and almost ferocious expression
of countenance, he had a most ungainly and uncouth figure,
which became more conspicuous if he appeared in the tight-
fitting uniform of the period ; consequently he hated a
uniform with a cordiality that seemed to be reciprocated.
The regulation coatee or · jacket never went on his back, for
he got a tailor to invent a coat which was a compromise
between a plain or ordinary dress frock and the regulation
uniform coatee.   On this singular and ludicrous garment—
which might have mystified the philosophic Herr Teufels-
drockh in *Sartor Resartus*—he stuck a pair of epaulettes of
enormous size.   When necessity, in the shape of public
duty, compelled him to appear in uniform, he donned this
coat, and, like our friend " H. B.," he was the cynosure of
all eyes.   If he was not exactly " the glass of fashion " or
" mould of form," he triumphed in being " the observed of
all observers," and many were the jokes and sly flings made
at his expense on his appearance by his friends and acquaintances, which were generally repaid with interest, for
Townshend was a thorough wit.   For instance, once at a
fair a group of the local magnates, composed of a couple of
J.P.'s, the resident physician, Mr. Sub-Inspector Townshend,
the rector, etc., were conversing in the street.   The rector,
the Rev. Mr. Henn, an " Aminadab Sleek " sort of person,
beneath which appearance he carried a sly, quick, and
cutting wit, used to delight in having a joke at Mr. Townshend's expense.   Here is a specimen :—

" Oh, dear me," said the Rev. Aminadab, rubbing down
and feeling Mr. Townshend's epaulettes, " what a martial
figure in uniform ! what an Adonis in face and figure ! I'm

sure Ajax must have looked like this when defying the
lightning. And what becoming and warlike ornaments
these epaulettes are! how silky the fringes!" rubbing them
down.

" Oh, I wish," growled Townshend, manifestly annoyed
at the badinage of the Rev. Aminadab, " that the devil had
them."

"Well, maybe *he has*," whined "Aminadab," looking up
into Townshend's face, which, indeed, had a rather fiendish
expression on it.

Here a roar of laughter drowned any further remarks, but
when it subsided the tables were turned on the Rev. Aminadab by Townshend's "retort courteous" touching the
possession of the epaulettes by his satanic majesty.

"No," roared he, "but he's feeling them!"

Notwithstanding Mr. Townshend's drawbacks and appa-
rent unsuitability for the position which necessity compelled
him to accept, he was a most invaluable officer to the
Government, for he was the most accurate and reliable
Government reporter at the monster meetings of O'Connell.
He was selected for this post of note-taker from the fact
that he was by profession a journalist, literary man, and
politician, coupled with a memory so tenacious, nay, almost
miraculous, that he could, without taking a note, repeat
verbatim from memory every speech that he heard. This
was an invaluable faculty at a time when Pitman's art was
unknown, or only in embryo. O'Connell held him in much
esteem, from the fact that he (Townshend) always reported
the proceedings and speeches accurately, and invariably,
when cross-examined at any trial that might arise, "never
had heard anything on which a prosecution could be
grounded, or anything uttered endangering the Constitution". The Liberator used always to shake hands with
him, and to introduce him to his colleagues, at all the
meetings, in a joking, bantering way :—"Gentlemen," he
would say, "allow me to introduce to your notice my particular old friend, Mr. Townshend. He's a good old Tory,
and what's better, an honest man, who has invariably reported
us accurately and fairly. He is not, gentlemen, an Adonis

in physique; neither was M. Robespierre, whom he is said to resemble very much, with this slight difference, that the tiger which Robespierre* was said to resemble, was pock-marked, whereas the animal Mr. Townshend claims resemblance to enjoyed an immunity from the effects of that disease."

This grim sally of Dan at Townshend's expense was provocative of much laughter, in which the worthy "Tig er" himself joined. When it subsided he always managed to turn the tables on Dan by some such remark as "Cork and Kerry men bandy with each other".

"Don't they call you 'Tiger Townshend'?" once commenced one Counsellor Murphy, who, from the violence of his manner of cross-examining a witness of the opposite side, got the sobriquet of "Bulldog Murphy".

"Ay," was Townshend's prompt reply, "and don't they call you 'Bulldog Murphy'?"

The most amusing story of "Tiger's" career in the force was as follows:—One day the dread news arrived at his office that the general in command of the Dublin military district was instructed to inspect the men under Mr. Towns-hend's command. The consummation devoutly to be wished by the heads of the Constabulary was that the men and their officer should be well up in drill, so that the general would be enabled to make a favourable report to the government of the efficiency of the police. If a bombshell had exploded in his office it could not have caused greater consternation than the arrival of that intelligence. Why Mr. Townshend's district of all others should have been selected was an enigma, and will ever remain so. Some astute persons averred that some one suggested to the general that he would have some

---

* The sanguinary Robespierre was a low-sized, sallow-complexioned, mean-looking man, deeply pitted with the small-pox. He described himself once in a letter to a lady who had written to him for his portrait in the following words:—"Madam, I cannot supply you with my portrait, but if you wish that I should assist you in forming an idea of my features, just imagine a Bengal tiger deeply pitted with small-pox, and you will realise them". The ferocious revolutionist was not wanting in grim humour. Mirabeau also suffered from small-pox, and after his recovery from the disease he was so horribly pock-marked that a relative described him as being "as ugly as the d——l".

fun if he just " got up " the inspection.   However, there was
no alternative but to prepare for the ordeal ; and poor
" Tiger " made a desperate resolve to master the problem of
putting his men through the manual and platoon exercises and
company movements.   At all the eligible cross-roads in any
sort of a central position the men of his district were assembled
every day for drill for weeks previous to the day appointed for
the general's inspection.   Mr. Townshend's " second in command " was an amusing old head-constable named Denison,
whose sole passion and taste was drill.   He spoke of nothing
but drill ; he thought of nothing but drill ; and he looked
with supreme contempt on anyone who knew nothing of, or
could not converse on, drill.   With this mentor, Mr. Townshend had high hopes of being able to cut a decent figure
when the general came.   Like a great many others old
Denison was unfortunately a sort of man who could show off
to great advantage when left to himself—" monarch of all he
surveyed "—but the moment a superior officer came on the
scene he could literally do nothing, and would break down
miserably, even in the simplest movements.

At length the eventful day approached, and never did a
prime minister weigh and deliberate a certain line of policy in
an impending crisis in the State with such deep anxiety as
did Mr. Sub-Inspector Townshend weigh between whether
he should follow the regular drill vocabulary, or stick to what
he called his " manœuvring," the explanation of which the
reader will find farther on.   Although well coached by
Denison in the mysteries of the intricate art and the incessant practice which had taken place from the first intimation
of the visit of the general, he had serious misgivings that he
would break down completely when it came to the great
man's presence on the drill-ground ; so the night before the
day announced he held a council of war with old Denison as
to the line of action he should pursue next day.

" I'll break down as sure as my name is Townshend," he
said.   " The devil himself invented drill, I verily believe.
I've mastered Greek and Latin easily ; I've read my 'Horace'
with delight, and every Greek and Latin author that ever
wrote ; I've written leading articles for my journal that made

skin and hair fly; I've read up, in the original German, Schiller and Goethe and Wieland and their contemporaries; but may everlasting oblivion obscure the name of the man who invented drill."

"Oh, heavens, sir!" exclaimed Denison, "is it possible that you hold the noblest, the grandest, and the most sublime science ever invented by all-conquering man in such a disparaging and contemptible light?"

"I do, Denison, for I believe the devil himself had a hand in it; for, look here now, say to-morrow I break down, I am considered a nonentity, notwithstanding that I may have done the most heroic acts in bringing to justice offenders such as murderers, burglars, robbers, pickpockets, etc., etc. However, that's not the present question. Shall I stick to the 'manoeuvring' or to the words of command? I'll break down as sure as my name is Townshend if I stick to the 'command'."

"Well, sir," replied Denison, "you're best judge yourself; but if you're not sure of yourself at the 'command,' maybe it's better to stick to the 'manoeuvring'."

Now the explanation of the question of "command" and "manoeuvring" is briefly this. By a very ingenious device, and with the help of a trained party of men in collusion, Mr. Townshend needed only to give one stereotyped word of command and the men would go through all the various evolutions of company drill, from the initiatory "present arms," as if they received the varied and proper words of command. This curious and eccentric system of drilling was the sole invention of "Tiger" himself to pull him through the ordeal of an inspection such as was pending over him. For instance, the manual exercise of the time commenced—"Present arms," "Shoulder arms," "Order arms," "Fix bayonets," "Shoulder arms," "Port arms," "Charge bayonets," "Shoulder arms," etc., etc. Now instead of following the various and proper words of command, Mr. Townshend commenced—"Manoeuvre number one," "Manoeuvre number two," "Manoeuvre number three, four, five, six, seven," and so on through all the movements. Of course the whole secret of the success of the thing rested with an intelligent company of men, and it has often been the case that a party of men have pulled their commander through, at an inspection by a superior officer, by not obeying when a blunder in the word of command was made, but following the proper movement. *En passant*, many a man has been pulled through at the Depôt, when on probation for promotion, by the reserve men on the same lines.

Next day Mr. Townshend and his party were assembled on the parade ground, anxiously awaiting the arrival of the general; and having warned the men that he'd stick to the "manoeuvring" as the safest plan, he gave them an hour's practice at it, much to his satisfaction and ease of mind. At length the great man was seen approaching, accompanied by the county-inspector, and when they arrived Townshend roared out—" Manœuvre number one !" instead of "General salute—present arms ". The men, in obedience to the command, presented arms with great precision. The general duly "returned" the salute, seemed somewhat mystified at the strange word of command, but said nothing, and requested the men to be brought to the "shoulder ". " Manœuvre number two," Townshend again roared in the voice of a Stentor, and the men in obedience brought their carbines to the "shoulder ". The general was manifestly puzzled at a repetition of the "manœuvring," but still asked no explanation. He then inspected the company, the ranks having been opened for that purpose by another "manœuvre " from Townshend, and at its conclusion requested Mr. Townshend to put the men through the manual and platoon (now the firing) exercise. " Yes, general," said Townshend with great *sang-froid*, and addressing the men he prefaced his "manœuvring" by warning the company what particular "manœuvres " the great man wanted performed, on the cogent reasoning embodied in the apothegm, " Forewarned is forearmed," which at this particular time was fraught with great importance to him. "Now, men, perform these manœuvres correctly :—Manœuvre number one, two, three, four, five, six, seven, etc." The men performed all the various motions with admirable precision, till both exercises were completed.

Now the general looked askance at the county-inspector as to the curious scene being enacted before him, of a body of men going through a large number of varied military exercises by virtue of one stereotyped, mysterious word of command. The " county," with all his anxiety for a favourable report and minute, could not help an involuntary smile appearing on his face at Townshend's " manœuvring," but refrained from giving any explanation of the matter to the general. At the conclusion of the manual and platoon exercises, the general expressed himself much satisfied with the steady manner in which they were performed. He then drew the county-inspector aside, asked him about the officer's curious word of command, and expressed astonishment at the admirable manner in which the men performed the movements notwithstanding.

" Oh, general," explained the county-inspector, " I must inform you that Mr. Townshend's was a political appointment ; never regularly drilled or trained ; was editor of a Conservative journal in the south of Ireland ; did yeoman service for his party ; became bankrupt in the general depression, and the Tories in return were bound to do something for him ; so they gave him one of the vacant subinspectorships, and here he is, a fish out of water, as he terms himself. He has a drill phraseology and system of his own ; civil body you know we are."

" Oh, I see," said the general with a faint smile ; " can he put the men, by this means, through any company movements ? " he asked.

" Certainly, general," replied the " county," who now saw that he might have confidence in Townshend's device to pull through the ordeal. " Mr. Townshend, the general requests that you'll put the men through some company movements ; and as you and your men have a system of your own, he doesn't mind what particular evolutions you go through."

" With pleasure," responded Townshend, " I shall feel happy in acceding to the slightest wish of the general. Men, the general desires me to put you through some company movements, and he's not particular as to what you do.

Now then, like one man, manœuvre number one, number two, three, four, five, six, etc.," and thus he went on as before, the men marching and counter-marching, advancing and retiring, forming square and "receiving cavalry," breaking into column to right and to left, forming fours in all their phases, rallying and skirmishing, and, in fine, went through all the various company movements of the period with as much precision as if the premier drill instructor of the Depôt had them in hand, and all by Townshend's magic "manœuvre" one, two, three, and so on up to fifty or sixty. The general manifested much curiosity at the singular display being enacted before him, and, after intimating to Townshend that he had seen enough to enable him to form an opinion of the efficiency of the police, requested that the men might be dismissed, and then he asked Mr. Townshend some questions touching his drill system.

"You see, general," explained Townshend, "I always find this the safest and best system with the Irish Constabulary; most intelligent body of men in the world; I invariably leave them to choose their own movements, and they're sure to be right. They are automatic; trained as if they were a machine, and I merely turn the handle, when they move with the precision you've just witnessed; in fact, they require no commander at all for that matter."

The general warmly complimented Mr. Townshend on his excellent manœuvring. "I wish," he said, "that our fellows could manœuvre half as well. I congratulate you, Mr. Townshend, on your splendid system."

During this interview between the general and Townshend the county-inspector could scarce contain himself with laughter, but by a free use of his pocket-handkerchief managed to conceal his risible emotions; and so the famous "review," as the men called it, ended.

Poor "Tiger" is long since gathered to his fathers, but in his time he represented one of the curiosities of the strange, eventful history of this island.

" BILLEY."

Head-constable William C——, whom I must include in
the category of eccentrics, was the smallest man in the force.
He was the son of the Reverend Robert C——, one time
rector of St. A——'s Parish, City of Dublin, who died comparatively early in life, leaving a family unprovided for. The
guardians of the deceased clergyman's family sought to put
the elder children to business, and selected a good house in
the city to which to apprentice the eldest, William, but they
found that he had conceived the notion and passion of joining the Constabulary—to them an eccentric and insane idea
—inasmuch as he was physically ineligible to join on account
of his diminutive size, being scarcely five feet in height and
slight in proportion. Nothing could dissuade him from his
determination of joining ; so, to smooth over difficulties,
some influence in high quarters was procured, and, to obviate
the difficulty of stature, he got a clerkship in the Constabulary office after his appointment as a sub-constable. He
held this for some years, till some new Constabulary Act
necessitated a change in this department, so that a number
of clerks had to clear out and take up their post in counties
as ordinary duty men. William got the rank of constable
(sergeant), and was sent to Tullamore, King's County. In
due time he was appointed head-constable ; and although his
diminutive stature impressed his guardians with the idea
that it was sheer quixotism for him to join the force, never
was a greater miscalculation made. Never was there a
man more suited to govern himself and others both above
and below him as " Billey," the sobriquet he was generally
known by in the province in which he served. His station
was considered a species of reformatory for refractory men,
and the bare threat of the county-inspector to unsteady men,
when going his rounds of inspection, of sending them to be
stationed under " Billey," was a good deal more efficacious
than a fine : " I'll send you to Head-Constable C——'s
station if I get another complaint against you." Sometimes
he would put it in a vague sort of way at stations where
trouble was being given by the men : " There's a man who

is familiarly known as ' Billey ' in this county; some of you men may know him and some may not; I find it necessary that some of you here *should* make his acquaintance, and if I don't *change* my mind by finding that a *change* has taken place in the manner of serving of some of you here, I'll give *someone* an opportunity of cultivating it." This threat was decidedly as effectual a deterrent as any that the draconic Code of Regulations sets forth for evil doers.

Now, one would imagine from this pen-and-ink sketch of Billey that he was a tyrant and a despot. There was not a scintilla of either one or the other in his composition ; on the contrary, he hated tyranny, and grappled with and worsted those in high positions that endeavoured to tyrannise. By the way, I have always looked upon the rank of head-·constable as the most peculiar and important of all the grades in the R. I. C. He is the " prime minister " who holds the power in his hands—that is, if he is made of the right material to hold it—and we have always looked on a head-constable, when promoted to a sub-inspectorship, as relinquishing his power and relegating himself to the region of effete authority. I have known head-constables wield the powers this "fulcrum " position gave them, with such signal effect that they became the terrors of those in high places, and to those in minor positions as well.

Now such a one was " Billey". Metaphorically and literally we might say he was the *enfant terrible* of his district ; not indeed that he had the least appearance of the " terrible " in his manner or bearing, for a more infantile, subdued, and undemonstrative little man one could not meet. He was never known to manifest anger, or in fact any emotion, notwithstanding that he might be abused by his superiors, or even his inferiors ; and he seemed a stranger to resentment. Whenever he had got a reprimand from headquarters he would laugh a little chuckling, scoffing sort of laugh, and call the whole station about him to read it aloud, when another man would have concealed his discomfiture from his subordinates. " Egad, I've got a lacerating," he would say ; " all come here till I read it for you," and then he would moralise on the matter for their special benefit and warning. " Now, men, mark me ; words are but wind ; see how the I. G. can do nothing to me but blow windy words at me on this file, because I don't leave it in his power to do anything else ; and do you not leave it in *my* power to do anything else. You can abuse me and call me plain ' Billey ' if you like, but the moment you step an inch out of the rules and regulation of discipline or duty, I'll have two fingers manipulating the pen on foolscap for your special reading, at the end of which you'll be writing, ' I admit the above charge,' or, ' I deny it,' as the case may be." After this short homily the little man would shuffle away to his office and be forthwith immersed in the mysteries of his returns and accounts.

.   There were two features about " Billey " that seemed to possess all the attributes which made him so formidable ; they were his eyes and the fingers of his right hand. Those organs seemed to concentrate in themselves that latent force that could awe a giant ; and many a Hercules of a sub-constable trembled at the combined action of both when he was found *in flagrante delicto* of some breach of the rules and regulations by " Billey ". The eyes, which were coal-black, had a dangerous kind of a dead man's stare, the fixed glare of a wax-work figure, which was not ruffled or disturbed by the faintest wink ; whilst the fingers, long and attenuated, worked with a pantomimic action, as if they were anticipating the writing of the report against the erring one. Indeed, many a man in a higher position than a sub-constable has felt the same terror of this fixed unwinking stare of " Billey's," and could exclaim with Macbeth at sight of Banquo's ghost—

> "Avaunt and quit my sight ! Let the earth hide thee !
> Thou hast no speculation in those eyes
> Which thou dost glare with !"

As an amusing instance of his manner of getting out of a difficulty, the following couple of instances will be worth narrating, viz.:—

There came to the district he was serving in a new sub-inspector and a new resident magistrate, their predecessors having been transferred " at their own expense," which is sufficient explanation to the initiated as to the why and wherefore ? Mr. D——, the "resident," was a stern, taciturn, cold, and haughty man, whilst the Constabulary officer was his very opposite. The former had all the attributes of the calculating and phlegmatic Saxon, whilst the latter was a fiery-tempered Celt, who came of a family whose fire-eating proclivities in the old duelling days of Ireland were notorious. With men of such opposite dispositions, who had to act together in their official capacities, it was not likely that an amicable feeling could last. Before long an inveterately antagonistic feeling sprang up between Mr. D—— and Mr. T——, which gave "Billey" a great amount of trouble. The district was much disturbed at the time, and bodies of police were scouring the country night and day. The magistrate would order "Billey" to do a certain patrol to a certain place ; the officer would countermand it and send him to another place. The magistrate would demand an explanation of "Billey" as to why he disobeyed his order.

"Have you sent the patrol where I ordered, head-constable ?"

"No, sir," replies "Billey".

"Why not, head-constable ?" demands the magistrate.

"My officer countermanded it, and named the townland of Ballyknockscatherum as the most disturbed place," was the answer.

"Once and for all, head-constable," says the magistrate sternly, "I warn you that if you disobey my order again, I'll report you. You and your officer are constables under my command in this district. I'll overlook the matter this time, but don't let it occur again. Send a strong patrol to Bally-knockdholdhrum ; there are greater probabilities of outrages from the 'peep-o'-days' there than at Ballyknockscatherum."

"Yes, sir," assents "Billey," and to Ballyknockdholdhrum the patrol is sent next night.

Next morning "Billey's" officer questions him touching the patrol to Ballyknockscatherum.

"Have the patrol found anything wrong in that townland I ordered you to send them to ?" he asks.

"They haven't patrolled to that townland, sir," is the reply.

"They haven't ! Why haven't they done so ?" sternly demands the officer.

"The order was countermanded by Mr. D——, who said that Ballyknockdholdhrum required the patrol more."

The fiery and impetuous T—— leaps up off his chair, flushed with anger, and thunders at Billey :

"How come you, sir, to disobey my order? How came you I ask," giving the table a mighty thump of his closed fist, "to obey the orders of a civilian, and to set at nought and defiance those of your officer? I've warned you repeatedly to attend to my orders, and this will be the last time I'll overlook your indiscipline. I'll report you if it occurs again."

"Well, sir," mildly pleads Billey, "I'm doing my best to carry out both your and Mr. D——'s orders. I'm placed in an unenviable position between you ; both of you threaten me with pains and penalties for disobeying your orders ; I am unable to define who I should obey ; but I must inform you, sir, I'll always obey the *last order I receive* for my own safety. If you countermand Mr. D——'s order, I'll obey you. If Mr. D—— countermands your order, I'll obey him, so between you be it. I may mention, sir, that it may be prudent for you both to abandon the course you are pursuing in your official functions."

This was anything but throwing oil on the troubled waters, for the officer hissed at Billey :

"Do you mean to convey a covert threat to me, sir ? If I thought it was concealed in the last portion of your speech I'd make you rue it."

"Oh no, sir," mildly remonstrates Billey, "only friendly advice, sir."

"Thank you for nothing ; keep your counsel and advice to yourself till I ask you for it," said the officer with withering contempt.

Now, this "friendly advice" of Billey's simply and plainly indicated that he was preparing materials for a report against one and the other of the officials. His subtle device of obeying the last order he received gave him a valuable safeguard of witnesses, in the shape of the patrols and the sergeants in charge of them. When the officer and the magistrate found that Billey's line of action was to obey the last order he received, they both made it a point to appear at the barrack or other assemby ground of the patrols at the hour they (the patrols) were to start on duty. Each official endeavoured to give him *the last order*, and so to triumph over his rival. It was a struggle in its way for ascendancy, and the two gentlemen laboured so industriously and pertinaciously, that they brought about as ludicrous a state of affairs as could be imagined.

The patrol of some fourteen men are "fell in," ready to start; Mr. T—— and Mr. D—— are there.

"You'll proceed, head-constable," orders Mr. T——, "with this patrol to Ballyknockscatherum, and lie in wait near Muloughney's, as there is a probability that the Whitefeet intend to attack him, and let a report of the state in which the place is found be made to me in the morning."

"Yes, sir," replies Billey; "right turn, men, quick march for Ballyknockscatherum."

"Hold! head-constable," thunders the magistrate; "didn't I order you to send this patrol to Ballyknockdholdhrum?"

"Yes, sir," replies Billey, "but didn't you hear Mr. T—— giving the last order?"

"Well, sir, haven't I repeatedly told you to obey my orders? It is I that am responsible for the peace of this district. Take that patrol to Ballyknockdholdhrum, and report to me in the morning the state in which it was found."

"Yes, sir; left turn, men, quick march for Ballyknockdholdhrum."

"Halt, men," thunders the officer. "Head-constable, haven't I repeatedly warned you against disobeying my orders? March that patrol to Ballyknockscatherum."

"Yes, sir; right turn, men, quick march for Ballyknockscatherum."

"Head-constable," roars the magistrate, "march that patrol to Ballyknockdholdhrum, or mark the consequences if an outrage occurs there to-night."

" Yes, sir; left turn, men, for Ballyknockdholdrum."

" At your peril, march to Ballyknockscatherum, and if an outrage occurs in it to-night and no patrol there, I know who'll be held accountable," yells the officer.

" Yes, sir; right turn, men, quick march for Ballyknock-scatherum."

And here a running fire of counter-orders abbreviated to 'scatherum and 'dholdhrum, 'dholdhrum and 'scatherum, are aimed at Billey, who is on the alert, like a watchful auctioneer for the last and highest bid, making the men turn to the right or the left like so many weathercocks in obedience to the variations of the wind. In fact the starting of a patrol was so ludicrously like an auction, that the men, quick to see the humour of the thing, used to have a cant phrase—" D'ye think, Tom, will we have an auction to-night?" asks Tim.

"Of course we will; sure it's the only fun we have," replies Tom. "Who d'ye think'll give the highest bid?"

" Faith I dunno; our officer has a thremindous voice, an' he's all fire an' tow; but, sure, Billey couldn't ketch who gave the last ordher in the ructions the other night, and asked the sargint and the men who did they hear givin' it. Sure didn't young Muldoon, the recruit, who thinks it's an auction, say that he heard the officer givin' the last bid."

" Begor, that's most laughable."

It will be as well to explain that Billey generally got the patrol off when the disputants commenced a wordy war with each other, and therefore ceased to countermand the respective destinations they ordered.

Those who knew Billey could forecast that an end to the scenes between the rival officials would come in due time, by observing the movements of the " writing fingers" that have been described before. Tom, one of the men on the previous night's patrol, remarked to his comrade Pat, " I'm thinking Pat, that there'll soon be an end to squabblin' between Mr. T—— and Mr. D——. Did you see Billey's two long spidher-legged fingers, the dangerous ones you know, workin' away all the time the 'auction' was goin' on yestherday evenin'?"

" Oh, in throth I did, Tom, an' I wish them luck over
the hills an' far away before long."

Billey's revenge on the two officials came some time after,
and he summed up his report with a crushing *prima facie*
case against them, which is the most amusing episode of the
whole business. It was petty-sessions day, and Mr. D——,
the stipendiary, having some writing to do, entered the
court-house an hour or two before the opening time, and
seated himself on the bench and commenced. Mr. T——
wishing also to write, and requiring a reference to the
petty-sessions books, entered soon after. Finding he required some elbow-room, and that Mr. D—— occupied the
middle of the bench, which was small, he said—

" Move your chair over a bit and give me room ".

This was unheeded by Mr. D——, and Mr. T——,
having his whip in his hand, gave the magistrate a smart
cut of it just along the thigh, accompanying it with the
remark—

" Do you hear me, sir ? Move your chair and give me
room."

The magistrate turned livid with rage at the indignity and
humiliation, and hissed out in a voice hoarse with anger—

" Yes, I'll move from the vicinity of one who, like the
upas tree, poisons and infects the atmosphere around him.
My bodily and mental health will be gainers by giving such
as you, and the family you spring from, a wide berth."

This, spoken with withering emphasis and scorn, was the
signal for retort, recrimination, and a raking up of family
blemishes—anything but a parliamentary style.

In the middle of the wordy *rencontre* the officer suddenly
remembered that a third person was present, listening to
everything, and *that* third person was Billey. He came
into the court with Mr. T——, having likewise some writing
to do. Prudence suggested to him (Mr. T——) that it
would be as well Billey should hear no more of the " reve-
lations," and said to him—

" Head-constable, leave the court and go over to the
office, and wait there till I come."

" Yes, sir," said Billey, and was proceeding out of the

7

court when the magistrate, to still assert his authority over
the officer, called him back.

"Come back here, head-constable, and remain in this
court under my orders. When you are here, or when I
direct you to do duty, you are under my command, as well
as *this other policeman here.*"

"Yes, sir," said Billey, coming back from the door and
taking his place as before.

"Go, sir," thunders the officer, "and await my orders in
my office. How dare you disobey your officer's orders?
I'll report you."

"Yes, sir," said Billey, again proceeding to the door.

"Come back here, head-constable," shouts the magistrate,
"or mark the consequences of disobeying my orders; I'll
report you."

"Yes, sir," was Billey's stereotyped acquiescence in the
"last order he received," and he came back as before; and
thus they had him, like a prize-walker, travelling to and fro
from the door to the bench at every "Go out!"—"Come
back!"—"Go out!"—"Come back!"   At length, seeing
there appeared to be no cessation of the "orders," he
changed his tactics, and going to the door of the court-house
he put one foot outside on the footpath and the other foot
inside the building, straddling his legs out as wide as his
little person could afford.   There he remained with one leg
in and the other out, like a miniature Colossus of Rhodes,
saying—

"Gentlemen, you've placed me in a dilemma—a very
unenviable position.   I am trying to obey you both; I am
tired of travelling back and forward.   The only way out of
my difficulty would be that one-half of me should go over to
the office whilst the other remained here.   That being a
physical impossibility, I am trying the nearest approach to it
in deference to your orders; so I have one leg out and the
other leg in.   With the leg that's out I obey my officer,
with the leg that's in I obey my magistrate; so, gentlemen,
you can have no charge against me for disobedience of
orders.   But I may as well inform you, gentlemen, that this
is the last occasion you'll make a shuttle-cock of me for your

rival battledores. I'll report you both to-morrow to the proper quarter ; " and then he pulled out an enormous note-book and commenced rapidly taking down the whole " Ches-terfieldian " dialogue *verbatim*, to be quoted hereafter. The contending officials had ceased for a few minutes their wordy war, attracted by his singular attitude, to observe him. During the lull they heard what he said ; but they shortly recommenced hostilities, which were only ended by the petty sessions clerk entering to announce the court open and to admit the public. The officer now descended from the bench, and, approaching the door, looked at Billey, who still maintained his " Colossus of Rhodes " position, writing away furiously.

" Come away out of that, head-constable," the officer snapped at him ; " quit that ridiculous position, and don't be making a fool of yourself."

" Am I relieved from it, sir ? " asked Billey. " I'll relieve my leg that's outside, which is the one I have caused to obey your order, if you tell me so ; but if not I'll remain here till the whole world and Garret Reilly sees me, to use a familiar saying. It is you two have placed me in it."

" Ah, trash ! " exclaimed the officer ; " I thought you had better sense. Come away out of that," and he walked rapidly away.

" All right, sir," said Billey, pulling in his leg, " that relieves me a bit. Now if my magistrate would relieve my inside leg I'd be obliged to him," and he still kept his leg in the same position.

The magistrate presently came down to go for a few minutes to his house to dress for the court, and shuffled past Billey without speaking. Billey seeing this called out after him :

" Hollo, sir, a word with you if you please ".

" Well, what do you want ? " said the justice, coming back.

" Are you going to relieve my inside leg, or am I to remain here ? If you don't relieve me I'll not stir out of this till dooms-day," replied Billey.

" Don't annoy me with your disgusting tomfoolery ; I've something else to do now. What do I care if you remained there till you'd rot," he snapped at Billey, and hurried off to be in time to take his place on the bench, so that the "locals" should not be "wondering" where the "paid" was, whilst they, the "great unpaid," were at their post.

"Humph," grunted Billey, as he looked after the retreating form of "the paid," "till I'd rot indeed. Very consoling, your worship; but I'm thinking, sir, *you'll* be rotting somewhere else out of this district ere long. Antrim and Kerry are far apart—the antipodes of the island—and probably you both will be making some explorations there if you have any taste for geology or antiquities;" and thus the little man soliloquised as he finished his notes, and then hurried off to march the duty men, prosecution men, prisoners, etc., to the court.

Next day, as Billey was writing in his office, there came a gentle rap at his door, and, on his responsive "Come in," there entered a reverend gentleman, oily, sleek, and radiant, as he beamed on Billey with seductive smiles.

"Good morning, head-constable; hope I don't intrude."

"Oh, not at all, sir, not at all," responded Billey. "Sit down."

"Oh, thanks; my business will be brief," continued the clergyman. "Ah, ahem ! I—I just called to speak to you about something I heard that occurred in the Courthouse yesterday between Mr. T—— and Mr. D——; some hot words; they threatened each other, and—and—and, I believe, gave you some trouble. Well now, you know, gentlemen *will* be gentlemen, and you know Irish gentlemen are peppery, and *will* have their hot-blooded evaporations; all vapour, smoke, you know; 'tis a good job for us, head-constable, that the days of our duelling are over, and that it is only 'words, words, words,' as Hamlet says to Polonius. I must inform you they are not going to report each other, at least Mr. D—— is not, and I hope that *you* won't make any report of the matter, and that it will drop. You know Mr. D——, and of course Mr. T——, would be both changed, perhaps to distant parts of Ireland, and wouldn't that be an awful thing? besides the disrepute it would bring on them. Dear me, how strange the position you're in, Mr. C——.

I knew your father, the Reverend Robert; we went to school together."

This last little stroke for Billey's sympathy and friendship was put in with the skill of an accomplished diplomatist, but his reverence might have kept it to himself as well as the rest of his special pleading, for all the chance it had of swaying the inflexible Billey from his purpose.

"Oh, indeed, sir," he replied, "there was a very ugly and unseemly scene between them. It is only the last of a series and I must put a stop to it; I have a duty to do and I won't flinch from it; I have my report now finished. They have trifled with me, and placed me in very unenviable positions. Did you ever, when a boy, play shuttle-cock and battle-dore?" he asked of his reverence.

"Yes, I did," was the reply.

"Well, that is a fair symbol or figure of the manner I was treated between them; I should not be surprised if the next thing they did was to get a pair of bats and make a cricket-ball of me. They've been making weather-cocks of me and of my men, facing north and south, east and west, as their high-mightinesses chose to blow their stormy orders at me, but, begad, I'll put wind in their sails before many days; I *will* report them."

"Oh, dear me, head-constable, do revoke your edict against them," pleaded his reverence; "you know we all have our infirmities," etc., etc., and so he went on, to no avail; Billey was not to be diverted from his purpose, and his reverence departed to inform Mr. D——, who had sent him on the diplomatic mission announcing peace on his side. He (the clergyman) had hardly left the house when another gentle rap at the door was heard, and there entered another diplomatist from Mr. T——, announcing peace on *his* side, but with a like result as regards Billey's "war policy".

The rest is briefly told. True to Billey's prophecy as to the result of his report, one was sent to the remotest northern county and the other to the farthest south. Billey did "put wind into their sails".

Billey's last and concluding piece of machiavellian strategy, in putting a tyrant *hors de combat* may be considered the most ludicrous and amusing incident of all. It is an axiom that power corrupts, and there is no more congenial domain for the exercise of tyranny than a body of men organised on a military or semi-military system. If a man in authority was naturally of a despotic disposition, he might with impunity gratify it to his heart's content. I used the word "impunity"; I should qualify it by explaining that there are times when it may be risky. I have seen young officers in a heated dispute about seniority and precedence, for the sole object of assuming command of a large party of police crossing from one railway terminus to another, through Dublin, *en route* home from the north to their respective counties. It was for the *éclat* and gratification of that craving for the "pomp and circumstance," of being seen by admiring citizens "in command," a pardonable vanity if it was bounded by a "show-off before civilians"—as the men phrase it—passing through a city. However, not to digress too far from the subject proper, there came, once on a time, to be stationed in the district where Billey, as "prime minister," acted with such subtlety, tact, and *finesse*, as a "practical politician," an officer who assumed the *rôle* of autocrat and iron despot in his little world of man and district. He was facetiously given the sobriquet of "Blood-and-Iron" by some ingenious individual, long before a certain continental statesman was dubbed with the same. Being "monarch of all he surveyed" in each little kingdom of Liliput that he ruled in, he was allowed to carry on his system of capricious tyranny unchecked, until at length it was *aut Cæsar aut nullus* with him. I remember a duke who owned the barrack coming to speak to him, and the guard, hurrying into his office, said—"Here's the duke, sir, an' he wants to see you". "Tell him to wait there till I'm ready. What a fuss you make rushing into my office! Go, mind your duty, sir." When he *did* see the duke he stuffed his hands into his trousers' pockets with a jerk as he approached to the nobleman, as much as to say—"I suppose you think you're a big fellow".

When "Blood-and-Iron" saw Billey, great was his wonder and contempt at the little handful of a man, and he treated him as an inferior being altogether. It is an idiosyncrasy, or rather a trick, of some officers to treat sergeants with studied and special contempt before their men, and "Blood-and-Iron" revelled in assuming towards Billey the most supercilious and insulting demeanour, which Billey meekly bore with the patience of a martyr or a stoic. But it was predicted by astute persons that Billey bided his time for his revenge, as the poet describes it—

> "The patient watch and vigil long
> Of him who treasures up a wrong."

Drill seemed to be an absorbing passion with "Blood-and-Iron". To be seen drilling a large party of men by admiring civilians was balm of Gilead to his vanity, and, to quote Hamlet's words, touching his prototypes of the mimic world of the stage, to "Strut and bellow and split the ears of the groundlings," seemed the climax of glory to him. He used to assemble the available men of the district, at various points, three or four times a week for the purpose of drill, and *that was* the memorable drill; such roaring, yelling, and abusing, for three, four, five, and even six hours, never had before astonished the natives of each rural *locale* where it took place. He was "loading" and "firing volleys," forming squares to resist cavalry, advancing and retiring, in column and in line, in fours and in files, marching and counter-marching, like the King of France and his army, "up the hill and down again," laying siege to some old ruined castle, and storming it at the point of the bayonet, and generally wound up the day's campaign by beleaguering some town or village and "capturing" it, marched in with flying colours, when he dismissed the men to return to their respective stations.

Now, many astute, knowing, people were wondering how long this would last, and how Billey bore being drilled so unmercifully all day, and, as a sequence, having to remain up to the small hours filling in his returns, and performing his clerical functions. When the men returned to their stations their remarks were both amusing and significant.

"Well, James, had yez a savare battle to-day?"

"Oh, in throth we had,· Mick; we laid sage to th' ould castle o' Rathmuck, an' routed the inimy, a lagion o' crows, jackdaws, an' owls. Divil a much more morodin the vagabones 'll have on the farmers' craps, an' the potatoes 'll be chaper for there'll be more o' them in the ground."

Here a roar of laughter greeted James' sally, who was a humourist in his way, and when the laughter had subsided he was further questioned :—

"Had yez many wounded an' kilt ?" Mick went on.

"Only one—ould John Barbour; the poor man in chargin' sunk in a soft part o' th' bog, on account of bein' so fat, like that ould fellow named Sir John Falstick, that Nowlan there does be readin' about in the new book he got."

Here another roar of laughter rewarded James ; but some of it was alloyed with the fun he evoked in his allusion to Sir John Falstaff, who it was manifest Nowlan had been reading about in a volume of Shakspeare, so, consequently, part of the laugh was at his (James') expense, and he continued—

"So we had great work pullin' 'em out of it, and the poor man had to be sint home in a canal boat that was goin' on a voyage in the direction of his station ; an' sure if he got home safe without bein' wracked he may thank his stars, for the night was very blusthry ".

This last sally convulsed the auditory with a concluding volley of cachinnations, which having been exhausted, Mick questions James further—

"Well, but did ye hear if Billey is plazed at this sort of work our high-flyer of an officer is goin' on with ? Is there any sign o' th' writin' fingers goin' to work ?"

"Oh, they can't make out, for ye see he has his carbine always in that hand, an' they say the dangerous fingers are a'most paralysed carryin' the carbine at the showldher for hours. I hear them sayin' that Tom Maloney endayvoured to watch them one day whin he got 'Stand at aise,' an' he seen the writin' fingers sthrivin' to work, but couldn't. But they say whin the fingers can't work the eyes is doin' it for them, for they have an awful starin' look."

"Oh, begorra, that's good news. There's a good sign in that ; he'll soon go to work."

True to the last speaker's forecast Billey commenced operations next drill day. Many a reader of these reminiscences must be familiar with those duck-pools skirting country roads, and mostly in front of farmers' houses; the colour of their waters is generally of that murky-yellow hue which accumulating deposits of mud, clay, and road-slush produce, with a green floating consistency about the edges; such, indeed, as Shakspeare terms "the green mantle of the standing-pool". Such a pool skirted the road where Mr. Sub-Inspector "Blood-and-Iron" was wont chiefly to carry on his drill operations, and every day there were three or four "marches past" it. Billey was observed for the last few days to look into it rather inquiringly as he filed past at the head of the column, as if calculating its depth. It was apparently very deep, and closely skirted the road. Some observant and astute men in the ranks could foresee that this duck-pool would shortly be the scene of some sort of operations on the part of Billey. On the day in question, as the column was marching past in fours, the carbine was seen to fall out of Billey's hand into the duck-pool, where it disappeared, whilst its owner marched on as if nothing unusual had occurred. A terrific roar, which was interpreted by the men to mean "halt!" was heard from "Blood-and-Iron," and when a halt was made that choleric officer rushed up to Billey, gave him a look that should have annihilated him, and then in a voice that should galvanize him into life again, said—

"What is the meaning of this, sir? Where is your carbine?"

"In the duck-pool, sir, or more familiarly known among the peasantry as the road-*shough*," meekly answered Billey.

"How comes it to be in the duck-pool, sir?"

"Fell out of my hand, sir."

"Fell out of your hand!" repeated the officer; "how came it to fall out of your hand?"

"Quite easily explained, sir," answered Billey; "you have paralysed my strength by keeping me at the "shoulder" for such an unusual length of time that my hand and arm are now so prostrated that they have refused to obey my will any longer; but the duck-pool received it very willingly."

Now this spoken by Billey so quietly, and with the little black waxwork figure stare fixed on the officer, seemed to arouse that choleric individual to an ungovernable pitch of fury, and he stamped and fumed.

"I'll dismiss or reduce you for this conduct," he thundered. "What a pattern you, a head-constable, are for the men. Go and pick up that carbine out of the water."

"I can't, sir," replied Billey.

"You can't," repeated "Blood-and-Iron". "Do you refuse to obey my order?"

"I don't refuse, sir," said Billey, "but you have paralysed my strength (temporarily I hope), so that you are the cause of my being unable to obey your own order. 'The spirit is willing, but the flesh is weak.' That is scriptural, sir."

"Take up that carbine I order; I'll give you one more chance of escape from the serious charge I'll prefer against you," slowly and emphatically continued the officer.

"I can't, sir," firmly replied Billey, keeping his basilisk eye fixed steadfastly on "Blood-and-Iron's" face.

"Enough," yelled that irate functionary, "I'll report you to the inspector-general. Go you (to a man in the ranks) and find that carbine in the duck-pool."

"Yes, sir," said the constable, who, it may be said, *en passant*, was a character in his way, or rather an oddity. He very systematically and methodically, after giving his carbine in charge to another, took off his belt and jacket, neatly folded them up, and gave them in charge also with instructions to take care of them, as if he was going to be executed and was giving his last injunctions.

The irate officer standing by, seeing the man making what he considered unnecessary preparations, snapped at him, "Hurry on, man, and don't be keeping us waiting".

"Yes, sir," said the man, as he proceeded to tuck up his shirt sleeves above his elbows very carefully and slowly. This done, he looked into the duck-pool like a person calculating the probable depth of a part of a river most eligible for the commission of suicide. After a considerable length

of time being spent in examining and calculating, he manifestly arrived at some conclusion as to his line of action, for
he went along the road a considerable distance and occupied himself seeking something in the ditch.

"What are you looking for now?" impatiently asked the
officer.

"Two big stones, sir."

"What do you want them for?"

"To kneel on while I'm sarchin' for the gun, sir; I can't
let my trousers be soiled."

"Come on but of that, sir," sternly ordered the officer,
"and don't keep me waiting here."

"Without the stones, is that what ye mane, sir?"

"Yes, that is what I mean; can't you search for the carbine without looking for stones to kneel on?"

"I can, sir," replied the man as he came towards the pool,
but instead of attempting a search, walked by it in through
the farmer's gate, and was just disappearing into the dwell-
ing-house when the officer, who was gazing after him, roared
out—

"Hollo! you fellow! where are you going now?"

"For a loan of a pitchfork, sir," was the reply.

"What do you want with the pitchfork?"

"To sarch for the gun, sir."

"Come away out of that, fellow, and obey my order; what
nonsense you go on with! Haven't you got your sleeves
tucked up, and what trouble is it to put your hand to the
bottom? Come along at once."

"Is it without the pitchfork ye mane, sir?"

"Yes, certainly; can't you get the carbine without a pitchfork? Such nonsense!"

"I can, sir," responded the "sub," as he walked back, and
as he approached his officer, he continued—"But sure,
whin you asked me if I couldn't sarch for it without the
stones, I said I could, because I knew Misther Mulrooney
within 'd lind me the loan of a pitchfork which 'd do as
well, an' sure if ye think the stones is betther I'll get them,"
and he walked by the pool and resumed his search for the
stones. During this scene the men of the company stand-

ing "at ease" were literally convulsed with laughter, but through fear smothered it as well as they could. As the officer looked after the "sub" resuming his search for the stones, he manifestly lost all command of himself and his temper, and screamed out, "Where are you going to now?"

"To get the stones, sir," he replied as before.

"Haven't I told you that you can pick up the carbine without the aid of stones?" said the officer.

"Well, I could, sir, but d'ye see if I kneel in that mud and slush I never could get my trousers clean, and it is my last issue, an' sure the county inspector might fine me for havin' it dirty, for he's very exact, so, if you let me get the stones to put my knees on it'll do me, an' if you think it'll be quicker, sure I'll get the pitchfork."

"If you don't obey my order this minute," roared "Blood-and-Iron," "I'll report you for gross insubordination and disobedience of orders. Take your choice now."

"Sure I'm not disobayin' yer ordher at all, sir, only sthrivin' to do mee best," pleaded the man.

"Do you refuse to search for that carbine?"

"Am I to sarch for it without aither stones or pitchfork, sir?" he again asked.

This was the last "straw" that overflowed the phials of the choleric officer's wrath, and he rapidly searched his pockets for his memorandum book and pencil, saying as he did so, "You've got your orders to search for that carbine and you refuse to obey me. What's this man's name and registered number?" the officer asked of the sub-constable's sergeant. "Patrick Oulahan, sir, number 10,784," replied the sergeant, and the officer took down very carefully the name and number, during which Oulahan commenced to take off his boots and socks, and then tucked up his trousers above his knees.

"Well, what are you going to do now?" asked the officer as he closed his book and saw Oulahan finishing his last operation and his legs bare.

"To go in an' sarch for the gun, sir," he replied.

"Is this fellow a fool or a rogue? One would think it was hydrophobia he had, it is so hard to get him into the water."

" He's only an odd sort of man, sir," replied the sergeant,
" and very careful of his clothes."

Oulahan now waded into the pool very carefully and put
down his hands to the bottom, groping about for Billey's
carbine, which, strange to say, seemed to have disappeared
most mysteriously, for Oulahan failed in finding its place of
lodgment at the bottom for a considerable time. Sometimes
he would make a grab as if successful, and exclaim, " I have
her now ! " and bringing his hand to the surface of the water,
would reveal some old used-up kitchen utensil, cast away by
the farmer's better half. Then he would stand upright from
his groping operations to make some inquiries of Billey as to
the probable place " she fell in," as if he was engaged search-
ing for the corpse of some one who had been murdered or
committed suicide. At length he found " her ". " Begor I
have her at last ! " he exclaimed, as he produced the carbine
with a beautiful coating of mud and duckweed wreathed
round it, " like a sea Cybele fresh from ocean," when the
duck-pool, " with its yellow waves, mantled her distress ".

" What'll I do with her now, sir ? " Oulahan asked, as he
came out of the pool with the carbine in his hand.

" Give it to the head-constable," said the officer.

" I won't take the carbine, sir," interposed Billey ; " I am
physically incapacitated from carrying it."

" What ! " shouted the officer, " you won't carry your own
carbine ! Do you refuse to carry that carbine ? " he fiercely
asked, as he produced his memorandum book again to note
every particular and minutiæ of Billy's rebellion, so that he
should make no mistake in the pending charges against him.

" I don't refuse, sir, if my physical powers admit ; but you
have paralysed my strength, and my hand refuses to obey my
will."

The officer now seemed to have closed all further parley
in the matter. Calling the men to " attention," he told a
man from Billey's station to wipe the carbine with a wisp of
grass and to carry it home, and then commenced the dismissal of the party to their stations, and so ended that day's
memorable proceedings.

Next day " Blood-and-Iron " sent a messenger from his

lodgings to say he required the presence of Billey at his rooms. Billey duly presented himself, and the following dialogue took place :—

Blood-and-Iron.—"Well, sir, what have you to say for yourself ? "

Billey.—" On what subject, sir ? "

B.-and-I.—" On what subject, sir !   Do you feign to be oblivious of the subject ?   You seem to take it coolly now, but perchance I might make it warm enough for you shortly."

Billey.—" I'm in a happy state of oblivion as to your meaning, sir, whether that meaning blows hot or cold."

B.-and-I. — " Well, sir, I'll blow it hot for you now on half-a-dozen sheets of ' foolscap ' I warrant you."

Billey.—" There's many a time something very hot loses its heat by radiation, being immersed in an absorbing medium —the air, water, ink, or some other fluid."

B.-and-I.—" You're impertinent, sir, also insubordinate."

Billey.—" Oh, no, sir, only scientific like yourself."

B.-and-I.—" To cut it short, what excuse or explanation have you to offer as to your outrageous conduct yesterday ? "

Billey.—" When and where, sir ? "

B.-and-I.—" When and where !   Oh, indeed your fencing won't do.   What excuse or explanation will you give the inspector-general regarding letting your rifle fall into the duck-pond and obstructing and thwarting the day's drill, by causing an unseemly and demoralising scene in presence of the assembled men of the district ? "

Billey.—" Oh, is that it, sir.   Well, then, I've none to give you."

B.-and-I.—" None to give me, sir.   Well, then, you'll give it to the inspector-general.   I'll report you for yesterday's proceedings."

Billey.—" Thank you, sir.   I'd be very happy you'd do so ; it'll just suit me."

B.-and-I.—" Just suit you, sir.   How do you say so when you'll be punished severely?   Will that suit you ? "

Billey.—" Not exactly to be punished, but to be reported."

B.-and-I.—" Oh, very well ; you'll have your wish with all my heart."

Billey.—" Thank you, sir. May I retire? I've some heavy writing to do."

B.-and-I. (after a pause).—" No, not yet. Now, I tell you what it is, on account of your position as head-constable, your family, and other considerations, I have concluded to overlook this serious breach of discipline on one condition— tender me an apology."

Billey.—" Oh, don't overlook anything, sir ; take my advice and report everything. It's the safest plan. I always followed the rule, and I couldn't be ever charged with neglect of duty."

B.-and-I.—" Well, surely you're the most singular person I ever met, head-constable."

Billey.—" Am I, sir? You don't really say so ; dear me ! "

B.-and-I.—" Well you are ; and now I have concluded to let this matter drop; for I perceive you are an eccentric person."

Billey.—" Oh, don't, don't, sir, for I am not going to let it drop. Take my advice and report everything. I always do it. I am going to report both yourself and me."

B.-and-I.—" What, sir ! report yourself and me ! What do you mean ? "

Billey—" I mean, sir, that I am framing charges against you regarding your attitude in this district since you came to it. You've been diverting me and the men from our more important and civil duties, harassing us, and exhausting our energies from our patrolling system, which is more important than your drill. We are not a military body ; from necessity we must be on a military model, and if we have to play at soldiers for our own safety, it doesn't come that we are to be turned into a mimic regiment, and go marching and drilling about the country this way, as if an enemy was on our shores. Excuse me, sir, but one would think you had a delusion that this was the Depôt, and that *you* were the adjutant. I advise you, sir, when you come to a county, to leave drill to the Depôt staff; it is their *forte*, ours is to detect crime. May I retire now ? "

B.-and-I.—" Stay yet *(blandly)*; I never met a man yet

to hold your position in the independent manner you have done ; I admire you for it ; tear your report and I'll tear mine."

Billey—" Oh no, sir ; I never do those things."

It will suffice to say that Billey put wind into Blood-and-Iron's sails, with a severe reprimand into the bargain. He had described the whole scene of the lost carbine, along with a graphic account of the officer's insane passion for playing at soldiers.

On matters of the duty of his district, and its freedom from crime and breaches of the law of any sort, Billey was always on the alert and efficient. His was a model district, and a law-breaker would think twice before he would attempt to commit an offence within the boundary of it. He was very zealous in detecting and punishing persons for cruelty to animals, and woe betide the adventurous cock-fanciers who would have the temerity to attempt a " main " within the domain of Billey. He considered it an indelible disgrace if the soil of his district were profaned by a cock-fight ; yet, after all, he was once an accessory and assistant at one of the largest " mains " ever fought in that part of the country—unknowingly, no doubt ; but the story is well worth telling :—

There was a great " main " organised by the cock-fanciers of three counties, and its programme was the subject of conversation of people far and near. The authorities, always on the *qui vive* to prevent such exhibitions, of course, got wind of the projected " main," and orders were issued to all districts to be on the alert and prevent it, so that the organisers found great difficulty in getting a place to " fight " in. They were hunted from one place to another by the police, and were on the point of relinquishing the project altogether, when one, Tom C——, an inveterate " cocker," hit on a plan of bringing the " main " off without interruption. He was a substantial shopkeeper from Billey's town and citadel, and seemed to know the " going of the guns " with Billey pretty well. He promised the chief organisers of the cock-fight that he would guarantee them as uninterrupted and pleasant a " main " as ever they fought, if they would leave the matter to him. He then proposed that they should, on a day appointed by him, fight the " main " within a stone's throw of his town. This proposal made them all stand aghast, for of all places they would never attempt a raid into Billey's district, let alone under his very nose, in the town-parks of his citadel.

" Will you leave it to me," said Tom, " and I'll keep my word."

"All right, Tom; go it. Desperate cases require desperate remedies ; we'll abide by you," they all chorussed, and a day was appointed for the meeting.

Now, the astute Tom knew that there is a little peculiarity —or rather an excusable ambition—existing in the force, to be foremost in getting information and detecting crime. The man who is the source and fountain of information in a station is an invaluable man to the public ; hence it is that a rivalry springs up which sometimes unfortunately confutes, mars, and negatives the very object that originates it—*i.e.*, the detection of crime. For instance, a gang of burglars are expected in a neighbourhood or a town, or coiners, or raids by local thieves on neighbouring farmers are apprehended, and each man of the district police is on the *qui vive.* Their officer's eye is on them, so is the county-inspector's. With-out extraneous aid it is almost impossible to get information, and each man has some "friend," a civilian, who is on the watch for him, and who is as anxious to catch the thief as the police themselves. When this individual has gleaned his information, he repairs forthwith to the barracks and asks to see *his man.* If the constable or sub-constable whom he seeks is not at home, he will not give his information to any-one else, for he has got his warning and instructions from his patron to communicate his information only to him, because it is obvious the others might reap the credit due to him ; the consequence is, the policeman may be absent so long that when he returns the information is too late—the mis-chief is done.

Now, Tom C—— knew that Billey had his satellite on the watch for the "main," and that the said satellite would only communicate his information to Billey, so he (Tom) had recourse to the following stratagem to out-manœuvre him.   He knew Billey had a chivalrous idea of the duties of his position as a public servant, which consisted in this— to be civil and urbane to all the Queen's law-abiding subjects, and by so doing impress upon them that the British constitution was the best, kindest, and most paternal of any form of government in the world.   This Tom knew to be a fundamental and orthodox principle with Billey, who was well known to step out of his road to oblige any one deserving of it, even to the extent of benevolently minding a trader's shop for a short spell if he were hard-pressed by business.

Tom, who was a bachelor, carried on his business without an assistant, and on the morning of the day appointed for the " main " he kept on the watch till he saw Billey coming out of his barrack and walk down the street.   As he approached Tom's shop, Tom rushed out with a letter in his hand, and hurriedly accosted Billey—

" Good-morrow, ' head '; fine morning, glory be to God ".

" Good-morning, Tom ; it is a fine day," responded Billey.

" Well, I'm in a fix and a dilemma, ' head,' " said Tom, opening the letter.   " Here's a letter of advice I got just now, telling me a large consignment of goods have been sent on to the railway station below, and I have to go and leave my shop to see after them as I require them forthwith for a large order I received from the Squire's, and I haven't a sinner to mind the shop whilst I go down with the cart for them."

" How long will you be away ? " asked Billey.

" Oh, only ten or fifteen minutes at furthest," replied Tom.

" Well, I'll step in and mind the shop for you," said Billey.

" Oh, thank you kindly, ' head,' " said Tom, a faint gleam of a cunning look of triumph in the corner of his eye ; " I knew when I told you my difficulty I had the right man. We're living under the most enlightened and paternal government in the world."   He then installed Billey behind

the counter in a chair, and producing a newspaper put it
into Billey's hand, saying—"There's to-day's paper, if you
care for it," and then stepped into his goods-cart and drove
rapidly off towards the trysting place of the cock-fighters.
In a short time a little field was crowded with "the fancy,"
among whom was one of the presiding magistrates of Billey's
petty-sessions town, a famous sportsman.

"Well, Tom, is all right? Any fear?" asked several.

"Not a scintilla ; not a jot," replied Tom ; "fear not my
hearties, Billey is safe."

"How did you manage it, Tom? What did you do with
him ?" chorussed a crowd of wondering sportsmen.

"He's minding my shop above, ensconced behind the
counter, and can't stir till I go back with a load of goods
from the railway," explained Tom, who received a salvo of
congratulations for his *ruse* with a babel of crowing from
the game combatants, and the "main" commenced and
continued for three-and-a-half hours, uninterrupted till its
close.

Now Billey's *confidante*, having discovered the progress of
the cock-fight, went immediately to the barrack and inquired
for the "head," and of course was told he was not in; so
he went away and returned after a time, but the "head" was
still *non est*, and again and again with the same result. As
he would communicate his information to no one else, of
course the cock-fight proceeded without the interference of
the police. The newspaper kept Billey pretty well absorbed
for a time, but he suddenly looked at his watch, found that
a half-hour had elapsed, and soliloquised—"What's keeping
this fellow?" he said—"ten or fifteen at furthest, and now
it is thirty minutes," and he strode from behind the counter
and peeped out to see if Tom was coming. An hour passed
and no Tom ; two hours, three, and yet the sound of his
goods-cart smote not on the anxious ears of Billey. "Look
at this work," he would say to himself; "wait till this fellow
gets me to mind his shop again. Could anything have happened to him? If I leave the place, it will be robbed. I
wonder, could I lock the door?" and he examined the construction of the shop door, and found it was only closed by

a thick wooden bar on the inside. At length Tom came back without having any goods. He was all excuses and humbleness.

"Oh, murdher, ' head,' I hope I didn't trespass on you too long, but it was inadvertent. Sure, what d'ye think but the truck containing my goods was left by mistake at the wrong station, so I had to go by the next train to look after it, and against I got back it was a long time, and the truck won't come on now till the night goods. Isn't this a poor case ; these stupid railway people are always blundering."

"Ah, then," said Billey, "when you get me to mind your shop again you'll see a white blackbird. Couldn't you send word by some one from the railway ? Maybe I am required at the barrack since."

"Oh, I hope not, ' head,'" said Tom consolingly. "Sure, there's no trouble going now ; the country is very quiet."

"Ah," said Billey, "but I hear there's a great cock-fight expected to come off somewhere in this county, and I don't like to remain away from the barrack very long, for fear the information should come to my sub-district in my absence."

"Oh, is it that cock-fight they're talking about ? Sure that is all over ; it *has* come off ; you may make your mind easy about that ; it'll trouble you no more ; it's all over long ago."

"Ah ! d'ye say so, Tom ? " exclaimed Billey, with surprise and curiosity manifestly awakened. "Where did it take place, did you hear ? "

"Well, I don't rightly know what part of this county," replied Tom.

"Oh, I'm glad it's over at any rate," said Billey, "for it gave me much trouble watching it, and I wish the police luck that didn't detect and prevent it ; the county-inspector *will* be talking to them about it and asking explanations. Good-day, Tom, I must hurry off."

"Good-day, ' head,' and I'm much obliged to you," responded Tom, and in an undertone, as he looked after Billey's retreating figure, "When the cat is away the mice will play ".

When Billey reached the barrack the guard reported that an individual had been several times at the barrack seeking him, manifestly having information of importance which he would communicate to no one but the "head" himself; and as they were speaking the same individual made his appearance. Billey rushed to meet him, and, drawing him aside, asked—

"Well, Jack, have you any news? I heard you were seeking me several times;" and there was a faint misgiving of something wrong expressed in Billey's countenance.

"Oh yis, 'head,' I was; it was about the cock-fight," replied Jack.

"What about it, Jack?" eagerly asked Billey, a gleam of suspicion now flashing on his mind regarding Tom C——'s goods-cart and protracted absence.

"Begorra, sure they fought the greatest "main" ever was known below, undher th' ould moat, an' undher yer very nose, an' all the money they say that was bet on the cocks was awful. I kem up here immediately to tell ye, but ye wor out, an' I kem several times, but no wan knew where ye wor. I'm towld the handlers an' heelers had a divil ov a fight—cut skulls an' bloody noses."

"How long did it last, do you know, Jack?" continued Billey, for the purpose of comparing the duration with the length of time Tom C—— was absent.

"Three an' a-half hours, I'm towld," replied Jack.

This answer increased Billey's suspicions, for it agreed to a minute, making allowances.

"Did you hear, Jack, who were the parties at the head of it?"

"Oh yis, I did," replied Jack, naming a lot of people, among whom was Tom C——; "and sure wasn't Misther D——, the justass o' the pace, there, naither more or less."

"What!" exclaimed Billey, "you don't say so, Jack!" and Billey brightened up from his despondency at the gleam of silver lining of the dark cloud hanging over him, for he saw that if called on for explanations as to how a cock-fight could take place under his nose, he could lay the whole blame on the magistrate who patronised it, and set him at nought.

To wind up, Billey was called on for explanations, and

came through the ordeal with flying colours ; but ever after he gave up his shop-keeping.

Billey's better half was a woman who was the very anti-thesis of her husband.   If Billey was a remarkably small man, she was a remarkably large woman.   She looked on Billey's machiavellian ways with ineradicable dislike, and many stormy scenes occurred between her and her lord, consequent on his stringent discipline.   Mrs. C—— was a portly and stately woman.   Much of her life had been spent in Dublin, where she imbibed a love for the drama.   Her great idols were Miss Fanny Kemble and her contemporaries of that far-off time.   She used to delight in talking of the glories of Crow Street and its long-faded triumphs in the histrionic world.   Many times she saved both policemen and recalcitrant civilians from Billey's clutches by holding him at arms' length ; for indeed he was but a child in her grasp.

"Man !" she would exclaim in Siddonian accents—"un-heroic, grovelling man—why do you stoop to such paltry ways ?   Have you no soul for what is noble or elevated ? Degenerate man, have you forgotten the family you spring from ?   The veriest peasant in your position would not do those things.   You come down the social ladder, they go up, and you meet on the same level ; but in heroic ways they go up, and you, you, contemptible man, come down."

"Very fine, indeed, ma'am," Billey would laughingly say, "but very inflated and redolent of the footlights.   The footlights wouldn't save me from a charge of neglect of duty, nor would all the wind you could blow into a bladder ward off the inspector-general's decision against me ; so let me go, ma'am, if you please ; I have a duty to perform."

With this notice I conclude my sketch of Billey, who, if he was strict, was no tyrant.   Light may the turf lie on his last resting-place, for he illustrated once more the truth of Pope's famous line—

"The mind's the standard of the man ".

With one parting anecdote I will leave Billey and pass on to the next subject.   Many readers of these reminiscences may be familiar with the name of a man who has left his footprints on the sands of Australian time and virgin soil. Bourke, the explorer of the Australian continent, whose statue now adorns one of the public squares of an Australian city, was a sub-inspector of R. I. C. before he departed for the antipodes. He, too, resigned his appointment to better his condition. It will be remembered that he lost his life in exploring the unknown interior of the vast southern island-continent along with some companions. Bourke, in physique, was a powerful young man, and his great feats as an athlete were the theme and conversation of all who witnessed them. As a weight, stone, or sledge-thrower, he vanquished all who competed against him, and, like most champions, he was ever on the lookout for "foemen worthy of his steel" and prowess. He chanced to replace Mr. Sub-Inspector "Tiger" Townshend, and in a neighbouring district Billey was located. Mr. Bourke had heard much of the *enfant terrible* of the county, but had not the remotest idea of Billey's stature, and, from the reputation of the man, Bourke fancied him to be of powerful physique. A few days after his arrival he said to his head-constable—

" This head-constable I hear so much of must be a powerful man. Is he a weight-thrower ? "

" Yes," answered the " head," who, by the way, was a humourist. " He never was vanquished yet in that department of athletics."

" Do you tell me so ! I'm glad to hear it. I'm thinking I'll take the shine out of him ; " and forthwith Mr. Bourke sent word to Billey that he would drop over and have a bout of weight-throwing with him.

On arriving at Billey's station he was so taken aback at seeing the diminutive man before him that he did not allude to the matter at all. However, he ever after laughed much at the matter that he should have put himself in training before going to his intended " tournament " with Billey.

" SARTOR RESARTUS."

Who can describe the torture of a Constabulary guard ? The military sentry is amusement compared to the police sentry. The soldier is two hours on and four off, *i.e.*, he is relieved every two hours, and he may sleep for four till his turn comes again. The Constabulary guard is twenty-four hours "on," and he is not relieved at all during that time. It is all very well in the daytime, but when night comes and sleep asserts her dominion, then comes the mental torture of the Constabulary guard. He endeavours to banish sleep, but the combat is in vain, and his fitful slumbers are accompanied by the most hideous dreams, arising from the fear and anxiety of being caught from within or without *in flagrante delicto*, in a serious breach of discipline. But this was in a bygone time, for now much of the rigours of guard are assuaged by an order of the late Colonel Wood, I.-G.

Tim O'Callaghan was guard one night in the station of a seaport town, and was aroused in the middle of a horrible dream, in which he saw the most grotesque and awful scenes of murder and robbery, by a loud knock at the barrack door. He jumped up precipitately, and hurrying to the door opened it, and although he saw strange and grotesque figures in his dream cutting each other's throats, the figure he now saw in his waking senses beat them hollow. It was apparently a man with a ghastly sallow face, a coal-black shaggy beard and long straggling hair, which gave an unearthly weird expression to his appearance; he was stark naked, and his body, legs, and arms were tattooed all over like an Indian's. He had on his back the door of a tenement-house, which he maintained in its position by keeping in a stooping posture, and by having a firm grip of the sides of it with his hands. Pinned round his middle was one side of the broadsheet of the *Freeman* newspaper; this and the door were the only articles he had in the shape of clothing. As Tim gazed on this apparition his hair stood on end, "like quills on the fretful porcupine," with terror, which was not allayed when the apparition began to jabber in an unknown tongue, at the same time pointing his long skinny finger to the door on his back. Indeed, to Tim at that particular moment Shakespeare's words touching the death of Julius Cæsar were forcibly illustrated—

> " A little ere the mightiest Julius fell,
> The graves stood tenantless, and the sheeted dead
> Did squeak and gibber in the Roman streets ".

This apparition squeaked and gibbered and gesticulated in a fearful manner at Tim, and its great dark eyes rolled terribly.

" The saints purtect us," ejaculated Tim, " what's this at all?"

He was answered by a fearful volley of jabber, in which the word "*banditti*" was often repeated.

" In the name o' heaven," said Tim, " what are ye at all? or have ye no nearer friend to appeal to but me?"

Another volley of gibberish, with more fearful gesticulation sergeant from the "apparition," determined Tim to call the in charge; so he went up and entered the sergeant's room.

" Are ye asleep, sargint? Sargint! sargint!"

" Who's that?" asked the sergeant, as Tim's last call awoke him.

" O'Callaghan," replied Tim. " Would ye get up, av ye plaze, sargint, as quick as ye can? there's the most awful looking thing ever I seen below at the door."

" What is it?" asked the sergeant.

" It's some sort of a fearful lookin' man, without a stitch of clothes on him except a door and a newspaper."

" A man without any clothes but a door and a newspaper!" repeated the sergeant, wonderingly.

" Yes," said Tim, " divil a ha'porth else he has on him but a door and a newspaper."

" In the name of providence," continued the sergeant, " did anyone ever hear a man telling such a story as this! How can a man have the door of a house for clothes? and you say he has a 'door on him'."

" I do, and I say it still," said Tim; " the only clothes I seen on him is the door of a house and a newspaper!"

Here the sergeant, who was sitting up in bed, groped for his box of matches, manifestly thinking that Tim was intoxicated. He lit one, and as it blazed up he scanned Tim's face closely to see if his suspicions were correct.

"Where has he the door and the newspaper on him, or what has he them on him for?" said the sergeant sceptically, eyeing Tim closely to see if he could detect evidences of lunacy in him.

"D'ye think I'd come up at this hour of the night to tell ye a lie?" replied Tim, feeling the sergeant's doubtful and suspicious tone and manner. "He has the door on his back, I suppose, to keep the rain off him, and the newspaper is pinned round his middle to keep the cowld off him, I suppose."

"According to that statement then," continued the sergeant with a sneer at Tim, "I suppose the door has sleeves to it and is buttoned round him. I never heard such a 'cock-an'-bull story'."

"Arrah, I don't care whether ye believe it or not," said Tim, whose temper, never the best, now boiled over at the sergeant's annoying scepticism—"I do my duty by reporting the matter to you, and you're in charge of this station."

"I'll be down after you," said the sergeant. When Tim got downstairs the apparition seized him, pulled him outside, and made fearful gesticulation at the number which was painted on the door, that was now resting against the wall instead of on the apparition's back. When the sergeant came down he was taken aback at the proofs of the truth of Tim's strange communication. He saw at once that the apparition had some object in bringing the door on its back to the barrack, and he communicated his suspicions to Tim that perhaps a crime had been committed, and that the door had something to do with it.

"Begor, you're right, sargint," said Tim, "divil a surer, but he must have been murdhered in the house that the door belongs to."

"Why, you goose, if he was murdered how could he be here with a door on his back?" said the sergeant.

"You're right," said Tim, and he laid his hand on the apparition's bare shoulder to satisfy himself it was a substance and not a shadow, so impressed was he that his strange visitor was not of this world.

"I see it at a glance; he's a foreign sailor, and has been robbed in the house this door belongs to. It's an ingenious device he has had recourse to. Number 15 is painted on it, and now to find that house is my move. Call up O'Rourke at once, and let him take guard for you while you come with me," said the sergeant.

The foreign sailor, for such the apparition proved to be, watched the sergeant and Tim closely during this colloquy ; and although he couldn't understand a word of English, he saw that the sergeant understood his case, and he gesticulated furiously at the number on the door. The sergeant examined the hinges, and found them of the old hook-and-eye pattern that would allow the door to be lifted off at will. When Tim was relieved by O'Rourke, the sergeant made signs to the sailor to take up the door and lead the way to the house it belonged to. That individual agreed to this with much evident satisfaction, and led the way to a remote part of the town, to a row of houses, the denizens of which were the worst characters in the place. At length they arrived at a doorless house where the sailor laid down the door. Without hesitation the sergeant put the inmates under arrest, and having searched the premises found the sailor's clothes, watch, and money hidden away in various parts. The unfortunate foreigner had been decoyed into it, and having been drugged he was stripped of his clothes and valuables; when he awoke he was forcibly ejected, stark naked, with only the newspaper he appeared in at the station. However, when all was quiet he went back to the door, and managed to get it off the hinges without attracting attention. He carried it on his back to the barrack, as *prima facie* evidence in the first instance, and in the next, that he could not make any mistake in swearing to the house he had been robbed in, and lastly that the police would find no resistance in entering without a search warrant. It was an ingenious device, and the sailor swore to the parties who had robbed him, and sent them "cruising".

But Tim's troubles on guard were not to end with this adventure.

On another night an "apparition" with another style of costume, appeared to him some time after the foregoing case. It was even stranger, and was, on Tim's first view, apparently a barrel with human legs and a head. It was an individual who had met a similar fate as the sailor, but instead of a door and a newspaper he only got a light barrel without either bottom or lid. Getting into it, he put his arms out through two bung-holes and made his way to the barrack. However, this individual's object in adopting the barrel as raiment was simply to supply the place of the fig-leaf, and was not a detective device.

When Tim saw what he thought was an animated barrel, he again ejaculated some pious exclamation, but his next thought was that his friend of the door and the newspaper had returned, and he said—"Hollo, are ye back agin ? an' is it a barrel ye have on ye now instead of a door ? "

"Policeman, I've been robbed of my clothes and money and I want your aid if you please," said the barrel's head in good English. This at once convinced Tim of his error, and he replied—"Oh, all right, wait till I call the sergeant ". He hurried up to the sergeant's room, and the scene between himself and that officer was as amusing, if not more so, than the first case of *Sartor Resartus.*

"Are ye awake, sargint ?   Sargint ! sargint !"

"What's the matter ? " grumbled the sergeant.

"Will ye get up if ye plaze ; here's another fellow without a stitch of clothes on him, only a barrel."

"Only a what ? " said the sergeant, seeming not to have understood Tim's words.

"A fellow in his naked 'pelt' with a barrel on him."

"A man with only a barrel on him for clothes," repeated the sergeant.   "In the name of all's above us, how can you call a barrel clothes ? How can he have a barrel on him ? What sort of a case is this you have now ? I don't know how it is, O'Callaghan, but you have always the strangest cases on guard of any man in the barrack ; you had a man with a door on him before, and now you have a man with a barrel."

"Well, how can I help it ? " said Tim ; "I didn't tell ye a lie. Come down and see for yourself ; he has his arms out through two bung-holes howldin' it on him."

"Oh, I see," said the sergeant, who, as before, took a

malicious satisfaction in scoffing at Tim, in revenge for being aroused out of bed by him—" I see, there's no sleeves to the barrel either, no more than the door; you had better send him to Jim Hoolihan the tailor to get them sewed on, as the holes for them are there."

" Ye needn't be cuttin' or sharpin' at me at all," said Tim tartly, feeling the sergeant's sarcasm directed at him. " I'm doin' my duty in reportin' the matter to *you*; he says also he was robbed."

" So, he's holding up the barrel on him," continued the sergeant as he proceeded to dress himself, " with his hands; there's no braces or suspenders to it; you ought to give him the second-hand pair you bought from O'Rourke the other day, as you have three pair now."

This "unkindest cut of all" at Tim roused him into a " retort courteous " on the sergeant, as he said leaving the room—" Well, I will if you give him the 'hand-me-down' top-coat ye bought beyant at the cast-clothes shop ". This parting " shot " of Tim's surprised the sergeant, for he thought no one knew where he bought the coat; but being a sort of man who could give and take a joke he laughed heartily at Tim's " retort courteous," and proceeding downstairs he found the barrel-costumed individual. Having heard the victim's story of the manner in which he was plundered, the sergeant told him to lead on to the house where it occurred.

It was a mid-summer's early morning, and day was making giant strides over the pall of night. People were beginning to be astir, when the novel spectacle of an animated barrel, with human legs and head, was seen wending its way through the township, " shadowed " by two members of the R. I. C. Some facetious individuals remarked by way of a solution of the mystery—" It is the perturbed *spirit* that once occupied the defunct barrel that is now 'revisiting the glimpses of the moon'; see how it examines each house to find the residence of those who had been most prominent in *murdering* it ". In fine, the robbed individual, although " native and to the manner born," failed in finding the house he was in search of, and the sergeant had to introduce him to the

county work-house temporarily, until his friends were communicated with.

THE SHAUGHRAUN OF THE CONSTABULARY.—" COLONEL " MAGUIRE.

By way of preface, before introducing a singular being,
whom I have to place in the category of the *Shaughrauns*, I
am obliged to make some observations on this class of wild
Irish character and Dion Boucicault's famous drama " The
Shaughraun ". Thousands of play-goers who have witnessed
the production of this drama may or may not have asked
themselves or others why the versatile Dion came to select
the singular, tatterdemalion, red-coated *Conn* for his hero.
Conn the Shaughraun is a distinct individual from the other
typical Irish peasants, *Shaun-the-Post* and *Myles-na-Coppa-
leen*. I remember once hearing in the Belfast theatre a
newspaper editor, who witnessed the performance of this
play for the first time, express great indignation and disgust
at the construction of the plot, on account of the vagabond
Conn being made the suitor and " intended " of the niece of
Father Tom. However, in my opinion, the founding of an
Irish drama on such a character, notwithstanding this blem-
ish, once more illustrates the well-known versatility and
prolific genius of Dion Boucicault. It is manifest from his
own account of the incident at Punchestown races, which
suggested the drama, and which forms the subject-matter of
a *brochure* he entitles " The origin of ' The Shaughraun,' a
Sketch from Life," that he was unaware that " Cantering
Jack," the original of *Conn the Shaughraun*, was only a type
of a class pretty numerous in bygone times in the south, east,
and west of Ireland. In this *brochure* Dion goes on to
describe " Cantering Jack " :—" He was a lithe boy of some
twenty years, dressed in a ragged scarlet coat and an old black
hunting cap, the cast-off suit of some whipper-in. One leg
boasted a top-boot, on which a rusty spur was tied about his
heel with a ' taste of cord '; on the other leg was the
remainder of a Wellington boot. His breeches were like
Joseph's coat, of many colours ; waistcoat and shirt he had
none. The attire, pulled any way about him, could not

conceal one of those model shapes that Ireland alone con-
tributes to the light cavalry of the English army.   Broad in
the shoulders, thin in the flank, his frame is what is vulgarly
called 'herring-gutted'; very long in the arms ; the hips, when
seen in profile, were broad, but narrow when seen in front ;
height, five feet eight ; weight, 150 pounds, and not an ounce
of fat at that—all bone and sinew.   Under a shock of brown
hair, a broad, beaming face defied delineation, for the features were constantly on the move; a mouth, vigorous,
large, full of gleaming teeth, seemed shrewd and mischievous,
over which two blue eyes, under long, black brows, were like
limpid wells of good nature and fun."   Such is the graphic
"pen-and-ink" portrait Dion draws of "Cantering Jack,"
who is but the type of a class well known in the old days
when hunting, racing, and stage-coaching flourished ; but
latterly it has almost disappeared.   "Cantering Jacks" were
not known among the people under the appellation "Shaughraun," although it is the proper one ; the name they were
familiarly known by was the somewhat curious one of "Count
the farmers," usually abbreviated to "Count".   The reason
of this was, that along with their other qualifications, such
as earth-stopping, knowing the cover where a fox was to be
found, carrying tired hounds, etc., they were supposed, when
called on by any gentlemen, to "count the farmers".   This
accomplishment must be considered the top of their qualifications, and it taxed the memory not a little.   It consisted of
calling over the names of all the gentlemen, squireens,
shoneens, and big farmers in the county, in a rapid manner,
giving to each name the genealogical tree and the good or
bad repute of the owner.   If the individual was in good
odour, a thorough sportsman, and generous with the *Shaughraun* and his class, he came in for great praise ; but if he
were a niggard, not favourable to hunting, and prevented
riding over his lands, he was held up to ridicule, laughter,
and scorn.   His appearance, family connections, peculiari-
ties, and genealogical tree were descanted on most unfavour-
ably, and he was represented as limiting his racing bets to
the ridiculous extent of "one shilling and nine-pence" and
no more.   I once saw one of those Bohemians endeavouring

to get into the presence of his Royal Highness the Prince of Wales at the Curragh races to "count the farmers" for his Royal Highness, but an attendant called on a constable to put him away.

Here just a few words touching the etymology, or rather meaning, of the word "shaughraun". Years before Boucicault's drama was written, we find Carleton—than whom there could be no better authority—explaining the term in *The Squanders of Castle Squander*, from which we learn that there were *shaughraun* school-masters in those times. In the opening chapter of that work he says :—

"The master of this school was a very remarkable man as an English and classical didactic. His name was O'Shaughraun, which signifies 'a man on the stray,' and indeed he was seldom off it, being a genuine specimen of the peripatetic as ere a learned vagabond in the records of old Greece itself."

There was a set of odd fantastic characters known about Dublin a good many years ago, one of whom, was the original of the "*Shaughraun*," Cantering Jack ; the others were called "Johnny Potts," "Saunders," "Hungry," and "Jingeldy the Coach". This last was a follower of stage coaches, and would run after the coach from the time it started in Dublin till it reached Cork or any other destination. He proved very useful to both passengers and coach officials, performing all sort of odd or miscellaneous jobs and services *en route*, for which he received some small sums by way of recompense. He seldom or never asked a lift, always scorning to take a rest by mounting the vehicle.

The Constabulary force, to be in keeping with other Irish institutions, has its *Shaughraun*, an individual whose history and life is, in its humble way, as strange and curious as any of the singular features which Ireland *par excellence* presents in contradistinction to England and Scotland. Outside the force this man is neither known nor noticed, but for the last half century he is familiarly known in the force as its courier, henchman, hanger-on, and *Shaughraun* all rolled into one. His strange life is not without its tinge of romance. Like the " Wandering Jew " of Sue's wild romance, this man has been ceaselessly wandering about Ireland nearly the whole of his life, never staying in one place more than one night. Over mountain and plain, bog and morass, through town and country, north, south, east, and west, including the coast islands, he has been found trudging to and fro for the last fifty years. The history of his strange career must be traced from a sanguinary episode in the "war of the Tithe," known as Carrickshock. The sanguinary encounter between the people and police, ending in the slaughter of the whole party of police and their ill-starred officers, with exception of one man who escaped by an artifice, was supposed to give the *coup-de-grace* to the levying of that most unjust and intensely obnoxious impost. The struggle ended by a party of innocent men being literally cut to pieces by the infuriated peasantry. The tithes were transferred from the backs of the tenantry to those of the landlords. There are many versions of the manner Mr. Gibbons, the officer and his men, fell into the ambush which ended so tragically for them; but I consider the narrative of the late ex-County Inspector Curtis the most reliable. He thus describes it in his *History of the Royal Irish Constabulary* :—

"On the 14th Dec., 1831, the most calamitous occurrence, connected with the collection of the tithes, in which the Constabulary were ever engaged took place. A process-server named Butler had several processes to serve for tithes due to the Rev. Dr. Hamilton. He proceeded on the above date under the protection of Chief-Constable Gibbons and thirty-six policemen to a place called Carrick-shock in the Co. Kilkenny, for the purpose of serving them. An immense number of country people assembled, called together by the ringing of the chapel bells in all directions. Having served two or three processes without molestation, Butler, with the police, was proceeding to a farmer's house through a narrow defile, with high banks on either side, upon the townland of Carrickshock, when they were suddenly set upon from the heights by upwards of two thousand persons variously armed, who only for a few moments ceased to hurl down their missiles, to demand the body of the process-server, and they would retire without doing further mischief.

9

This of course was refused, when the attack from behind walls and ditches upon the tops of the heights was renewed. Stones of a large size were hurled from above, wounding and knocking down many of the unfortunate men, who, from their position, could take little or no effect by firing upon their assailants, protected as they were by the rising ground. The police now fired a volley at some of the men who appeared more prominently upon the face of the hill. By this volley two of the country people were killed; but it was a signal for a simultaneous rush upon the constables, who were now unloaded to a man. A furious and overwhelming attack was made upon them hand-to-hand with sticks, stones, pitchforks, scythes, and reaping-hooks, and a complete slaughter of almost the entire party was the result. Fourteen of the men with Mr. Gibbons were barbarously murdered on the spot, and eight badly wounded, including Butler, the process-server, who, with two of the wounded police, died on the following morning; the rest succeeded in making their escape."

Mr. Curtis did not mention or allude to it, but it is asserted to be a fact that Mr. Gibbons met the fate of Mazeppa—that he was tied on the back of an unbroken colt, which was let loose and wildly galloped away. The last earthly sound heard by the ill-starred officer

> "Was the wild shout of savage laughter,
> Which on the wind came roaring after."

The subject of my present sketch, the *Shaughraun* of the Constabulary, was the son of a sergeant that was numbered with the slain at Carrickshock. After the death of his father, the shock of which somewhat turned his brain, he refused to adopt any species of employment, but became a wanderer from barrack to barrack, and eked out a precarious livelihood among the men by making himself a species of walking parcels-post, carrying from county to county all sorts of miscellaneous articles, such as musical instruments, walking-sticks, parcels, books, belts, and all species of accoutrements, etc. In the old times of sixpenny-letter-charge and coaching days, before railways and parcels-post were thought of, or were only in embryo, the *Shaughraun* was invaluable to the police. His integrity and strict honesty were so established that men used to trust him with more valuable property than the articles just enumerated. Often did he convey from some young "sub" the rent to the father, in some far distant county, to keep the old place over the family's head. Sometimes a horse, pony, cow, or jaunting-car was purchased and given to the *Shaughraun* for delivery at the far-away old homestead. I once saw a "sub" going home on furlough on his own car, with the *Shaughraun* in the driving-seat. The vehicle and horse were purchased for a present to his (the "sub's") father, and as the residence was remote, the *Shaughraun's* services were indispensable to find the road home. Sometimes the *Shaughraun*-courier did a stroke of business for his patrons, by disposing of the cow, horse, or pony at large profit, and instead of delivering the animal, he produced the money doubled or trebled. Once he was conveying a handsome pony, bought for five pounds, in a north-western county, by a young "sub" for his father, in far-away Wexford. In passing through Carlow one of the leading landlords of that county, seeing the animal, offered the *Shaughraun* fifteen pounds for it. That individual responded by naming twenty, and for twenty pounds the pony changed hands, the money being duly handed to the old farmer instead of the pony. But this was in bygone days, and latterly the *Shaughraun's* occupation in this extensive line is gone. I remember him some thirty years ago, when *en route* from far-distant Antrim to Kerry—a little, squat, wiry, active man, mounted on a shaggy Shetland pony, having an assortment of all sorts of nondescript articles on its back, behind and before the rider. He entered each barrack on the way, as if he was an authority, delivered his messages, and "inspected," after which he started again. This line of life compels him to be perpetually on the road, so that he has visited every police post in Ireland innumerable times during his life. It is his humour to assume a "rank," and for that purpose he dubbed himself "Colonel Maguire, Inspicthor-Giniral," and adopting the official phrases, his

visits to each barrack are "an inspiction". For the amusement of the party he performs a species of travesty on the
functions of the superior officers : "examines" the barrack,
"falls the men in," and "parades" them and goes through
the drill, makes his "entries," etc. He also retails all the
latest news and *on dits* of the force, promotions, pensions,
marriages, transfers, deaths, etc. Like the *Shaughrauns* of
the hunting establishments he used to wear a cast-off suit of
uniform, .but latterly he has discarded the practice, with the
exception of donning a forage-cap whilst he is "inspecting".
Having a tenacious memory, he, like his prototypes of the
red-coats, goes rapidly over interminable rolls of names of
inspectors-general, county and district inspectors, head-constables, sergeants, etc. The officers almost to a man know
him, and are for the most part liberal towards him, his
history probably being known to them. The late Colonel
Wood knew him well, and one day opposite the Depôt gate
pointed him out to a gentleman, saying—

"Do you see that strange-looking little old man standing
there ? Well, that individual has been visiting every police
station in Ireland for the last forty years. Come here, my
man," he said to the *Shaughraun*. "Have you visited
every station in Ireland ? "

"Av coorse I have, cornel," replied the *Shaughraun* in
his· broad Munster brogue. "What am I an inspicthor-
giniral, like yerself, for av I wasn't to inspict mee stations an'
do mee duty ? "

"Perfectly right, my man," said Colonel Wood, "but I
want to tell you there is a station you never put your foot
in."

"Name it, cornel."

Here Colonel Wood named a station so inaccessible that
it was with great difficulty he himself penetrated to it, and
he couldn't imagine how the *Shaughraun* could accomplish
it.

"Arrah, cornel, avourneen, I was in that station inspectin'
whin ye wor only a recruit in th' army. I'm yer sanior
officer on the list, an' I'll tell *you* a station ye never wor in,
an' mind ye, it's neglect o' duty av ye, cornel, an' av ye

admit id I'll only fine ye five shillins, but av ye aggravate id
bee denial I'll fine ye ten, cornel."

At this sally of the *Shaughraun*, Colonel Wood and his
gentleman-friend laughed heartily, and the former said—
" Well, my man, name it ".

And the *Shaughraun* named a certain station which he
knew that Colonel Wood was never in, and he gave proofs
of the *bona fides* of his assertion by reminding him that
stress of weather prevented a visit to it, to which " charge "
Colonel Wood, much to the amusement of his friend,
admitted, and paid the *Shaughraun* his " fine ".   However,
the inspector-general now in his turn demanded proofs of
the truth of the *Shaughraun's* assertion that he (the *Shaughraun*) was in the inaccessible station by naming the sergeant
in charge and his men.

" If you're not able to name the party on your last visit
there, I shall name them for you, and shall fine you five
shillings for making a false statement."

The *Shaughraun* had the sergeant and his five men's
names pat at his fingers' ends.   It was a well-known fact
that so tenacious was Colonel Wood's memory, that he used
to stand with his back to the regiment he commanded when
on parade, and from memory alone call out the roll of the
soldiers' names from beginning to end, and so he thought to
outwit the *Shaughraun* on that score.

The *Shaughraun's* way of life is now fallen into the sear
and yellow leaf, for he is nearing fourscore ; and now the
old man totters on his weary trudge from station to station,
and raves away about being pensioned off; how much he
will get for his fifty-four years' service ; where he will settle
down—" Och, och, but I think it time now to retire ; I'm
on the road inspictin' fifty-four years, an' I think I'll rest
now.   I'm going since '31, the battle ov Carrickshock, where
mee father was kilt.   Well, maybe they'd consedher some
day.   An' to look at all I seen pinshioned off, an' dead, an'
gone, an' to see me still in the sarvice an' the age o' me.
Och wirra, but it's a wairy time to look back at, goin', goin',
goin', for ever like a ' willey-th'-wisp ' or a wondherin Jew."

Well, yes, the poor *Shaughraun will* be " pensioned off,"

and he will " settle down " after his " long service " in that haven where the " weary are at rest," and where " thieves cannot break in and steal ".

" VI ET ARMIS."

It is amusing and curious to observe the mystification and astonishment of foreign visitors and strangers to Ireland, when they are told that the Royal Irish Constabulary are the police of the country. They can scarcely be brought to reconcile the identity of the military *tout ensemble* of the Irish *gendarmerie* with the prosaic civil constable of the sister countries, and stare in blank wonder when by chance they get a glance at a party of R. I. C. fully equipped and accoutred. I remember once when proceeding to the north, on entering a railway carriage with three or four of my companions, we were jocularly greeted by a gentleman, who, I subsequently found was a stranger, and who was the sole occupant of the compartment, with the exclamation—" *Vi et armis !*"

"Yes," I responded, but rather our dictum should be— " *Cedant arma togae !*"

" Volunteers ? " he queried. " I didn't think there were any in Ireland."

" No," I replied, " not exactly.".

" Rifle regiment, probably ? "

" No."

" Militia ? "

" No."

" Yeomanry ? "

" No."

Here he paused apparently puzzled, and at length he asked what arm of the land forces we belonged to, and I cannot forget the look of astonishment he gave at our accoutrements when I said we were police.

The most able and accomplished officer I ever served under was one whose profession was that of a civil engineer. In defending his own or his men's actions in any paper combat he " floored" all antagonists, no matter how affluent or powerful such persons might be. To quote the expressions touching him by a brother officer—" H—— delights in a fight on paper ; his style is so logical and his facts are so stubborn that they are literally and figuratively 'paper pellets of the brain ' ". He was great in times and places of tumult and riot, and he rose to the occasion in a way that was in marked contrast to many who lose their heads, notwithstanding that the manner he issued his orders savoured somewhat of the ludicrous, if not quixotic. He carried this eccentric style of giving orders into every minutiæ, even to substituting the military and naval phrase " mutiny " for that of the Constabulary "insubordination ". One night, on an occasion when a party of sorely fatigued and harassed men were sleeping in a temporary barrack, which for the uninitiated reader I must explain is termed a " straw-lodge," Mr. H——, in his anxiety and zeal for the peace of the agitated town, wanted a strong patrol, and told the head-constable to call up a number of men, who, on being aroused, grumbled and murmured, and feigned such prostration, that the head-constable went out of the building and told Mr. H—— that he could not get the men up out of the straw ; whereupon that accomplished but eccentric officer set up, in the most terrific and appalling manner, the cry of " Mutiny ! mutiny ! mutiny ! mutiny !" which so alarmed the recalcitrant "subs" that they jumped up, with the agility of harlequins in a panto-mime, and proceeded on the duty. Indeed this *penchant*, nay craving, after the *éclat* and glamour of the military command is not confined to Mr. H——. It pervades all men and all ranks to a great extent. Early in my service I remember an amusing episode, in which a sergeant who was smitten with the military mania, and five young "subs," myself being one, were the actors. The sergeant was left with his party to keep order in a village, a short distance from a town where an election of a member of Parliament was proceeding. Word was sent to the " straw-lodge " by a woman who owned a public-house, that some men were quarrelling and fighting about the payment of a round of drink, and requesting the aid of the police. " Yes," responded Sergeant Mac——, assuming a grandiloquent tone and attitude, "and I'll let them see *my way* of dealing with them. No humbugging or 'palavering' with me, I warrant you. Fall in, men, put on your appointments! put on your appointments, and look to your ammunition and your cold steel, and obey my command, and I'll show you how I'll put to flight those fellows." We "fell in" and marched with great precision to the "public," and having arrived just opposite the door, Mac—— shouted in a terrific manner— "Halt! front! with ball-cartridge load!" We duly obeyed the order, and when accomplished he gave the order—"Fix bayonets!" which was also performed with the usual amount of rattling, flashing, and clicking. These operations were viewed by the occupants of the "public" with manifest dismay and alarm. When he had his five men ready to his satisfaction, he approached the door of the house and announced in awful tones, that if they (the rioters) did not disperse forthwith he would "blow down," not only the "public," but the whole row of houses, with their occupants, "in one red burial blent". "I'll give you," said he, "three minutes, at the end of which, if you are found on these premises, I'll keep my word." Now this awful announcement caused the utmost consternation within. The proprietress set up a *whililew*, and divided her outcry between appealing to the sergeant for a respite, and showering a volley of abuse and anathemas on the erring ones—

"Oh sargint! sargint! for all the saints in heaven sake don't rack and ruin the poor lone widdy; get out o' mee house, ye vagabones, ye blaguards o' the world, ye dirty boccachs".

These individuals were no less alarmed at the prospect of so speedy an exit from this great stage of life, and made the most precipitate stampede from the bacchanalian temple.

The brawl being thus settled by Mac's *vi et armis* system, when he found that there was no need of "blowing down" the "public" and the whole row of houses, in the same pompous manner he gave us the command—"Shoulder arms—right turn—quick march—right countermarch—left countermarch," etc., which, to the uninitiated, caused us to strut up and down in front of the "public" for some time, till at length he marched us off to our quarters in the "straw-lodge," with as much pomp, as if he had a whole park of artillery at his command, to "blow down" all and every obstacle.

CHAPTER IV

A HUNT FOR A SKELETON.

" Can such things be,
And overcome us like a summer's cloud,
Without our special wonder."—MACBETH.

To enable my readers to fully realise all the surroundings of the following incident, I am compelled in the first instance to enter into a few short descriptive accounts of the romantic region in the County Sligo, which was the scene of it, and then to dip into some passages in Irish history, which will take us back through the dim mist of centuries to the very dawn of Irish recorded lore.

Some five or six years ago I was sent to take charge of Castlebaldwin station, in the Riverstown district. I did not exactly know for some time the great interest attaching to the country around, not the least being the scene of Carleton's most ambitious work, *Willey Reilly*; but I gradually came to discover that my sub-district was the most interesting historical spot in Ireland. It consists of the country and mountains round and about Lake Arrow, which rests placidly in a great elongated basin, studded with a "gay young group of tufted islands born of her". On either hand of the lake are situated the mansions and demesnes of county gentlemen, the most extensive being that of Colonel John Ffolliott, D.I., of Hollybrook, the lineal descendant of that "Squire Folliard" of Carleton's famous novel. Rising from the northern bank is Moytura Mountain, the most historic spot in Ireland, inasmuch as it was the scene of the two earliest battles ever fought on Irish soil between the *Firbolgs* and *Tuatha-de-Danaans* for the mastery of the island. A little to the west of the lake, and just where it finds outlet by a sluggish river, is the townland of Heaps-town, so called from an enormous monumental cairn, or simply a vast heap of stones, in a green field, the property of Captain M'Ternan, R.M. At the base of Moytura Mountain there is one of the largest *cromlechs* in Ireland, an enormous rock, as big as a house, reared on pillar stones. It is called by the peasantry *Lhabby Diarmud,* or the " bed of Dermod and Grana "—In O'Daly's *Munster Poets* we read (p. 46)—" Diarmuid O'Duibhne eloped with Finn M'Cum-hal's wife, Graine or Grace—*Leaby Dhiarmuid agus Ghrraine*—the bed of Diarmuid and Graine. The idea is that one of those extraordinary structures was erected every night during their flight in order to sleep upon. They never remained two nights in the same place ; and as Finn's pursuit lasted a year and a day, there must have been 366 beds erected."

The summit of Moytura mountain abounds in monu-mental remains, and the whole neighbourhood presents proofs of the great struggles that, in the dawn of Irish history, took place there. Ever since the late Dr. Petrie drew attention to this district by his celebrated lecture delivered before the members of the Royal Irish Academy in 1836, it has been the cynosure of the eyes of Irish scholars, archæologists, and antiquarians. The last lecture on the site was delivered by Professor Hennessy, Tod lecturer, before the members of the Royal Irish Academy, about a year ago. *En passant,* just a few words about Hollybrook :—The ancestral home of the Ffolliotts, and the scene of Carleton's best novel, lies on the southern margin of Lake Arrow, and is a beautiful and romantic demesne, made more attractive by the contiguity of Lake Arrow, which it skirts. The mansion is surrounded with beautiful grounds, the most attractive feature of which is the famous, unique, and unparalleled Box-tree Walk. To give an adequate idea of this phenomenal development of the box-tree, brought about by long years of culture and care, I would ask the reader to imagine two rows of box-trees quite close to each other on either hand of a long path six feet wide, the trees rising like poles to the height of forty feet, their foliage forming a thick and impenetrable hedge for the full height, trimmed and clipped as level as a wall. The clipping has to be done by means of scaffolding and ladders, and so thick is the screen that the wind blew down a large section of it some few years ago. Along this walk, tradition says, Reilly used to glide when approaching the house where his dear *colleen bawn* awaited him. On looking at this astonishing walk, one is forcibly reminded of the feasibility of the somewhat apparently improbable situation in which Shakespeare in " Twelfth Night " places three of his characters. It will be remembered that he conceals Sir Toby Belsh, Sir Andrew Aguecheek, and Fabian in a box-tree. Maria tells them (Act ii., Sc. 5), " Get ye all three into the box-tree : Malvolio is coming down this walk," etc ; and the question might arise as to how a box-tree could conceal three men. It is very probable that Shakespeare must have seen something similar to the Hollybrook box-walk, for it could conceal hundreds of men from observation effectually. There is a magnificent view of the lake from the front of the house, which is surrounded with rows of colossal beech-trees.

The memory of Willey Reilly and his story is not yet obliterated from the mind of the peasantry around, and it is said that Colonel Ffolliott possesses a portrait of him and the Colleen Bawn of his romantic love. The colonel by the way is an eminently popular gentleman amongst his tenantry and neighbours. As a landlord, he is loudly praised. He has scarcely ever evicted a tenant ; on the contrary, when any of them became impecunious and embarrassed, he advanced them loans to tide them over their difficulty. In winter he throws open his woods for the use of the poor people to get firewood ; and it is only when they go too far, by taking the " ell " when they get the " inch," that he looks after their doings in his woods. With these few remarks on Hollybrook, I will pass on to the

" PYRAMID " OF HEAPSTOWN.

" A sermon in stones."—SHAKESPEARE.

In the middle of a green field, the property of Captain M'Ternan, R.M., rises a colossal heap of stones that excites the wonder of all who see it for the first time.   The stones average about twelve inches in diameter, the largest being about twenty inches and the smallest about six or seven, and are for the most part round and smooth.   It is manifest that in rearing this enormous cairn, the pyramidal form was roughly aimed at.   Unlike the great strand cairn in the same county, there is no record or trace as to who this stony monument was raised over.   Beranger, who visited this region in 1769, in the course of compiling the work he was employed at, says it is the tomb of Olliol, King of Connaught ; but this is probably a mere vague allusion founded on no tangible grounds ; possibly he means Olliol Ollum, King of Munster.   It is fairly established that the great strand cairn has been reared to commemorate the fall of either Eochaidh,* King of the Firbolgs, who, after being pursued by the *Tuatha de Danaans* from *Magh Tuireadh* (Moytura), was killed by the three sons of Neimhidh on this strand or Cuchulin, who, according to M'Pherson's " Ossian," were killed here also—

" By the dark rolling waves of Lego, they raised the hero's tomb."

What Dr. Petrie's opinion is touching it I cannot say, as I was unable to procure a copy of his celebrated lecture on the antiquities of this locality ; neither have I seen the latest lecture on the same subject delivered some time ago by Professor Hennessy, on account of the rule precluding lectures, etc. from being published inside a year from the date of their delivery.   A workman who was employed excavating at the base of the cairn told me he saw great square blocks and flags arranged as if a sepulchre was formed beneath the heap.   If it be that the Danes rifled the monuments and shrines of Ireland, they must have penetrated beneath the cairn and carried away the remains of the individual whom it commemorates, so that even the dust as well as the name is gone, and the words of Byron touching a classic monumental mound is applicable to this stone-heap—

* The Very Rev. Canon O'Rourke, P.P., Coloony, in his *History of the Parish of Coloony*, holds that it was raised over this Eochaidh.

> '' Their flocks are grazing on the mound
>   Of him who felt the Dardan's arrow :
> That mighty heap of gather'd ground
> Which Amon's son ran proudly round,
> By nations raised, by monarchs crown'd,
>   Is now a lone and nameless barrow !
>   Within—thy dwelling-place how narrow !
> Without—can only strangers breathe
> The name of him that *was* beneath ;
> Dust long outlasts the storied stones,
> But thou—thy very dust is gone ! ''

It is likely that the accumulation of the stones must have extended over centuries, which illustrates in a literal sense Milton's lines occurring in his '' Epitaph on Shakespeare ''—

> ''What needs my Shakespeare or his honour'd bones ?—
> The labour of an age in piled stones''.

It is amusing to hear the curious traditions extant among the surrounding peasantry touching the cairn, the most popular being that the stones appeared in one night, and that they fell from the sky in a downpour, as a miller lets down a quantity of corn out of a loft. Here we have Othello answered when he asks—

> '' Are there no stones in heaven
> But what serve for the thunder ? ''

It is devoutly believed that there was not a single stone in the field at nightfall on the mysterious date, and that to the wonderment of the whole country they appeared in the morning. Another theory is that there was an Irish king, who, having heard of the pyramids of Egypt, left it as incumbent on his subjects to raise one that should dwarf those of Cheops or Chephren.

Pinkerton, in alluding to the Celtic custom of piling stones after this manner, says in his *Enquiry into the History of Scotland*, vol. ii., p. 14 :—'' Ancient monuments of the British Scots there are none, save cairns of stones, used as sepulchral memorials. These were adapted to Celtic indolence, while Gothic industry raised vast stones instead of piling small ones.''

How there can be lack of industry in a people who collected and raised this vast cairn is to me an enigma ; rather,
it might be said, the Celts were inferior to the others in
mechanical skill, but surely not in industry.

Of late years, the cairn has been greatly diminished in
size, from the great drain on its materials for the purpose of
building bridges, walls, sewers, houses, etc., and would have
in all probability disappeared altogether were it not that
Captain M'Ternan, R.M., much to his credit, put a stop to
the practice. And here, curiously enough, a stanza from
" Childe Harold " is applicable to it—

> " A ruin—yet what ruin ! from its mass
> Walls, castles, half-cities, have been rear'd,
> Yet oft the enormous skeleton ye pass,
> And marvel where the spoil could have appear'd.
> Hath it indeed been plunder'd or but clear'd ?
> Alas ! developed, opens the decay,
> When the colossal fabric's form is near'd,
> It will not bear the brightness of the day,
> Which streams too much on all, years, man, have reft away."

The most amusing version of the use and origin of the
cairn is the following. It was told me by one Tim Byron,
a name which, by the way, is pretty numerous in parts of
Sligo. Tim was a character in his way, and had a good
stock of local lore. He told me how he " heerd tell of Lord
Byron, his great namesake, an' that he was a rattler at
makin' poetry, an' was proud of him ". At the same time
he asked me if I knew or had heard tell of one Mick Merrick, a local bard, to which I replied in the affirmative, as
previously to my coming to Castlebaldwin I had made Mick's
acquaintance, and got specimens of his poetic effusions.
Mick had also "heerd tell" of his poetic namesake, Merrick,
and also Herrick, whom he contended was one and the same
man as Merrick, from whom he claimed to be a lineal descendant ; but more of Mick hereafter.

" Well, Tim," I queried, " what's your opinion on the
heap ? Do you think the stones appeared all in one night
as everyone thinks hereabouts ? "

" Arrah, bladdher for them, sargint ! what do they know about it ? Sorra ha'porth. Here's the raal cause of them bein' there, an' I can tell ye it'll do a dale o' good for all the poor onforthonate sinners that th' owld boy'll think he'll have at the day o' judgment. There was an owld king in Ireland a thremindious number o' years ago, an' he was a terrible owld man for fightin' and squabblin', and thievin' and robbin' his naybours, an' never looked after his sowl at all. Well, sir, whin he got very owld an' feeble, and seein' that his ind wasn't far away, he got very onaisy about what ud become ov him whin he'd die, an' was always ruminatin' how he'd get out o' th' clutches of owld Nick at the day o' judgment. Well, begorra, sir, he hit on a plan that he thought ud save himself an' all other poor crathurs from owld Nick, the vagabone. Ye see they wor great stone-throwers out of slings in those times; sure didn't Misther Downs, the most larned man we have, that lives there beyant a few miles away, tell us how Balyower o' th' evil eye was kilt bee a lick ov a stone out ov a sling. Well, the king ordhered his sons to put in his coffin, whin he was dead, his best slings, an' to make his subjects gether all the roundest an' handiest stones in all Connaught, and hape them over his grave, so as that, at th' day o' judgment, he'd have lots of stones for ammunishion to let fly at owld Nick, an' knock saucepans out ov him, an' that he wouldn't have to be runnin' about lookin' for stones. An' that's th' raison th' stones are round an' handy to fit in the sling, an' ye may depind on it, sargint, agin that hape is pelted at the devil (here Tim looked towards the cairn), he won't be in much humour to make his charges agin poor sinners ; an' don't ye see that although the hape is there thousands o' years there's no grass or clay betune thim to give trouble whin they're wanted."

Tim wound up his "theory" of the cairn by giving me a knowing look and wink, as much as to say, "there's the real simon pure about the heap of Heapstown"; and having now wound up my notes on this interesting portion of Sligo, I will take my readers back into the night of time through the *Annals of the Four Masters.*

The *Annals*, p. 17, vol. ii., go on to say *—"The age of the world 3303.—The tenth year of the reign of Eochaidh, son of Erc ; and this was the last year of his reign, for the Tuatha-de-Danaans came to invade Ireland against the Firbolgs ; and they 'gave battle to each other at Magh-Tuireadh in Conmacne-Cuile-Toladh in Connaught, so that the king, Eochaidh, son of Erc, was killed by the three sons of Neimhidh, son of Badhrai, of the Tuatha-de-Danaans, Ceasarb, Luamh, and Luachra, their names. The Firbolgs were vanquished and slaughtered in this battle. Moreover, the hand of Nuadhat, son of Eochaidh, son of Edarlamh (the king who was over the Tuatha-de-Danaans), was cut off in the same battle. The aforesaid Eochaidh was the last king of the Firbolgs. Nine of them assumed kingship, and thirty-seven years was the length of their sway over Ireland.

" The age of the world 3310.—This was the seventh year of Breas over Ireland, when he resigned the kingdom to Nuadhat after the cure of his hand by Diaucecht, assisted by Creidne, the artificer, for they put a silver hand upon him."

The excellent note to this passage explains about the hand thus : "It is stated in the battle of Magh-Tuireadh, and various other accounts of the Tuatha-de-Danaans, that Creidne Cerde made a silver hand for this Nuadhat, and that Diaucecht, the Æsculapius of the Irish, fitted it upon him, from which he was ever after known by the name of Nuadhat-Argetlamh, *i.e.*, Nuadhat of the Silver Hand. It is stated in the *Leabhar-Gabhala* of the O'Clerys that Diaucecht and Creidne formed the hand with motion in every finger and joint, and that Miach, the son of Diaucecht, to excel his father, took off the hand, and infused feeling and motion into every joint and vein of it, as if it were a natural hand."
—See O'Flaherty's *Ogygia*, part iii., c. 10.

* I have to acknowledge my indebtedness to Professor Hennessy, Tod Lecturer, Royal Irish Academy, and Record Office, Four Courts, for his instrumentality in procuring me access to the manuscripts and books in the " Academy," which afforded most of the historical notes I required to quote here ; also to Mr. MacSweeny I must tender thanks.

" The age of the world 3330.—At the end of the twentieth
year of the reign of Nuadhat of the Silver Hand, he fell in
the battle of Magh-Tuireadh-bh-Fomarach by Balor of the
mighty blows, one of the Fomorians."

The note S, *Magh Tuireadh-na-bh-Fomarach* goes on to
explain this passage thus: "This name is still remembered in
the country, and is now applied to a townland in the parish
of Kilmactranny, barony of Tirerrill, and county of Sligo.
There are very curious sepulchral monuments still to be
seen on this battle-field, of which a minute description has
been given by Dr. Petrie, in a paper read before the Royal
Irish Academy in 1836—See note C under A.D. 1398.
There was also a long account of this battle of the northern
Magh-Tuireadh, as well as of that of the southern Magh-
Tuireadh, or Magh-Tuireadh-Conga already mentioned, but
the editor never saw a copy of it.   O'Flaherty, who appears
to have read it, stated (*Ogygia*, part iii., c. 12) that Balor
Bemen or Bailclemnich, general of the Fomorians, was slain
in this battle by a stone thrown at him by the son of his
daughter, from a machine called *tabhall* which is believed to
have been a sling ; and that Kethleun, the wife of Balor,
fought with desperation, and wounded the Dagda, afterwards
King of the Tuatha-de-Danaans,* with some missile weapon.
This Balor, the general of the Fomorians, is still vividly
remembered by tradition throughout Ireland, and in some
places they frighten children by his name ; but he is more
vividly remembered on Tory Island, where he is believed to
have chiefly resided, and on the opposite coast of Donegal,
than anywhere else, except, perhaps, at Cong in Mayo."

Annals, p. 21, vol. ii.—" The age of the world 3331.—
The first year of the reign of Lugh Lamfhada [Lewy of the
Long Hand] over Ireland."

The age of the world 3370.—"After the fortieth year of the
reign of Lugh Lamfhada over Ireland, he fell by MacCuill

* Touching this name a writer says :—" This name, according to some
antiquarians, originated from the *Tuatha Danaans* being divided into
tribes.   The nobility, so called from *Quatha*, a lord ; the priest from *Dee*,
God, as being devoted to the service of heaven ; and the *Danans*, poets or
bards, from *Dan*, a poem.

at Caendrum. It was in the reign of this Lugh that the fair of Tailtean was established in commemoration and remembrance of his foster-mother, Tailte, the daughter of Maghmor, King of Spain, and the wife of Eochaidh, son of Erc, the last King of the Firbolds."

The explanatory note U goes on to explain this passage thus : " *Tailtean.*—Now Teltown, near the river Boyne, in the county of Meath, and nearly midway between Kells and Navan. This fair, at which various games and sports were celebrated, continued down to the time of Roderick O'Connor, the last monarch of Ireland. It was celebrated annually on the first of August, which is still called Lugh-nasadh, *i.e.*, Lugh's fair, games, or sports, by the native Irish."—See Cormac's *Glossary.*

Annals, p. 763, vol. iv.—" O'Connor Roe and Mac-Dermot marched with a great army against the Clann Donough of Tirerrill, until they arrived at Magh-Tuireadh, where they committed great depredations. The Clann Donough and Murtough, son of Donel O'Connor, with all his forces assembled, came up with them, and a battle was fought between them, in which O'Connor (Roe) was defeated, and Sorly Boy MacDonnell and his people were killed."

The explanatory note to the foregoing passage goes on to say : " *Magh Tuireadh.*—There were two Magh-Tuireadhs (Moy Tuirrys) in Connaught, famous for battles fought on them between the Firbolgs and Tuatha-de-Danaans, the one near Cong, in the County Mayo, called the southern, and the other, which is the one here referred to, in the barony of Tirerrill, county of Sligo, and called the northern Moy-tuirry. It lies in the parish of Kilmactranny, in the barony of Tirerrill, and is divided into two townlands, one called Moytuirry MacDonogh, and the other Moytuirry Coulan. Tradition points out this as the site of a dreadful battle between the Tuatha-de-Danaans and Fomorachs, and many giants' graves are shown, in which the heroes who fought there were interred. O'Flaherty describes the situation of the northern Moy-Tuireadh thus (*Ogygia,* p. 176) : " *In confinibus Tir-Olillae in Sligo et Tir-Tohilla in Roscommon agro*".

And Charles O'Connor of Belanagare, who lived for a long time near this place, has clearly and satisfactorily defined the situation in the following words :—"'The Fomorians invited back the Belgians to their assistance, and their conjunction produced the second battle of Moyturey, near the lake of Arrow (Lough Arrow), but distant from the former Moyturey about fifty miles, and, by way of distinction, called Moyturey of the Fomorians. This place, surrounded by high hills, great rocks, and narrow defiles, was pitched upon probably by the weaker side, but which made the attack is not recorded."—*Dissertations on the History of Ireland*, p. 167.

At this stage I deem it necessary to draw my readers' attention to Lugh Lhamfhada, king of the Tuatha-de-Danaans, one of the most celebrated characters of ancient Irish History. His name occurs in connection with the most famous men of comparatively modern times in Ireland. For instance, the *Annals*, at p. 1621, vol. v., in alluding to the death of the famous Shane O'Neill, go on to state :—"Grievous to the race of Owen, son of Niall, was the death of him who was there slain, for that O'Neill, *i.e.*, Shane, had been their Couchobar in provincial dignity, their Lugh Longhanded in heroism, and their champion in time of danger and prowess".

The footnote says : "*Lugh Longhanded.*—He was a king of the Tuatha-de-Danaans, and is much celebrated in ancient Irish historical tales ".—See *Ogygia*, part iii., c. 13.

In O'Curry's *Manners and Customs of the Ancient Irish*, p. 251, Lect. XII., allusion is made to the evil eye as follows :

Magh Tuireadh.—In the heat of battle, a Fomorian warrior and chief, named Balor, was dealing fearful destruction among the Tuatha-de-Danaans, not more by the sword and spear than by a certain natural (or rather very unnatural) gift which he possessed. This was no other, says the tract, than an evil eye which he generally kept covered, but to the effect of which he gave free range in battle. (And here may be observed an example of the manner in which supernatural powers were ascribed in these historic tracts, just as Homer frequently attributed to the more destructive heroes whose feats are described, as if to account for their intolerable superiority.)　Among those who were struck down by the power of this evil eye were Nuada (of the silver hand) himself, King of the Tuatha-de-Danaans, and the Lady Macha, daughter of Ernma; after whose death it appears Balor closed the magical eye again.　Thereupon the champion of the Tuatha-de-Danaans, Lugh (of the long hand) perceiving what had happened, dauntlessly went up, we are told in the tale, to the fierce warrior, whose fatal eye was at this moment closed, and denouncing his cruelty, threatened him with instant death.　Then Balor, hearing such taunts and threats, proceeded to raise the lid of the evil eye; but no sooner did Lugh see the movement of the lid, than he darted a sling-stone, says the ancient writer of the tale, at the eye, and, accurately attaining his mark, drove it through his enemy's skull; and this terrible Balor fell dead among his people. In this passage it is not said, however, that it was from a sling the stone was cast, but only it was a "sling-stone," a *lic-tailme;* and whether or not Lugh alone of all the warriors engaged in this battle was acquainted with the sling, we have no satisfactory means of determining, unless we admit the value of the negative evidence in the fact that no further allusion to it is to be found in this ancient tract.　It is proper to observe, however, that in the *Book of Leinster* we are told that it was with a stone from his sling, "*tabaill,*" that Lugh killed Balor (who was, we are told in this version of the story, Lugh's own grandfather).

There is a short but very curious ancient poem still in existence, which gives an extravagantly romantic account of the origin and composition of this very sling-stone by which Balor's evil eye was destroyed; from which it appears that it was an artificial composition, a "*tathlum,*" or conglomeration. The following is a literal translation of the passage :

> "A Tathlum heavy, fiery, firm,
> Which the Tuatha de Danaan had with them,
> It was that broke the fierce Balor's eye,
> Of old, in the battle of great armies.

> "The blood of toads and furious bears,
> And the blood of the noble lion,

The blood of vipers, and of osmuins' trunks ;—
It was of these the Tathlum was composed.

" The sand of the swift Armorial sea,
And the sand of the teaming red sea ;—
All these, being first purified were used
In the composition of the Tathlum.

" Brian, the son of Bethar, no mean warrior,
Who on the ocean's eastern border reigned ;—
It was he that fused and smoothly formed,
It was he that fashioned the Tathlum.

" To the *hero, Lughaidh,* was given
This concrete ball *—no soft missile ;—
In *Magh Tuireadh* of shrieking wails,
From his hand he threw the Tathlum."

O'Flaherty in his *Ogygia* tells us that in this battle there fell also Breas (who was deposed to make room for Nuada of the Silver Hand), Nuada himself, Ogma (inventor of the Ogham characters), Granien, and Kethlen.

* It was such a missile that, tradition says, caused the death of King Connon MacNessa, who was contemporaneous with Christ. The death of this Irish monarch is an episode that stands unique and unparalleled in the history of the Christian religion. The story is extant and familiar in Irish history, and the substance of it is as follows :—
The king was struck in battle with such a concrete ball as that described in the poem, and it sunk so deep into his skull that all efforts of his physicians to extract it failed. He did not succumb, however, but lived for years with it in his brain, and the physicians warned him to avoid all excitement or ebullitions of passion which, if indulged in, would endanger his life. He obeyed the warning until the day of the Crucifixion, when he asked a druid the cause of the awful phenomena of the darkness of the heavens. The druid replied that it was because of the cruel death of the Son of God on the Cross. " And what has the Son of God done that He should suffer thus ? " asked the king. " Nothing but good," replied the druid. This so excited and enraged King Connor that he drew his sword, and rushing out into a wood hard by his palace, he commenced to hew and hack the trees in a furious manner, lopping off great branches with mighty blows, exclaiming —" This is how I'd punish the murderers of the Son of God if they were here ! " The warning of the physicians being forgotten in his excitement, the concrete ball embedded in his brain performed its fatal function, for in the climax of his rage King Connor Mac-Nessa fell dead, the first individual to yield up his life for the Christian cause.
There is a belief prevalent among Irish historians that it was not a druid but a Roman Consul at the King's Court that informed him of the Crucifixion. T. D. Sullivan makes this incident the theme of one of his finest poems.

Again we find this Lugh Lamfhada alluded to by an ancient writer in connection with the mysterious and celebrated Goban Saer (*Goban Architect*). Of all the ancient Irish celebrities of any class or degree, there are none whose names are as familiar as household words in the mouth of Irish posterity as this extraordinary character. Throughout the length and breadth of the island, oral tradition supplies stories and anecdotes of the Goban Saer and his twelve journeymen; and yet his nationality, parentage, and history are involved in impenetrable mystery; mere conjecture and surmise alone is the extent that even ancient writers must confine themselves to regarding him and his history. Dr. O'Donovan speaks of him thus :—

"I have already alluded to the historical evidences which prove that the Goban Saer was no imaginary character or creation, however legendary the memorials of him may be considered; and I may here add, that it would appear from a very ancient authority, namely, the *Diunsenchus* preserved in the *Book of Lecan and Ballymote*, that he was the son of a skilful artisan in wood, if not in stone also; and that this artisan was, if not a foreigner, at least very probably of foreign extraction, and thus enabled to introduce arts not generally known in the country; and further, that the Goban himself was born at Turvey, on the northern coast of the County of Dublin, which, it is stated, took its name from his father, as being his property, and which, as he was not a person of known Milesian origin, it is but fair to infer he received as a reward for his skill in mechanical art. This passage, the text of which is corrected from two passages, is as follows :— 'Traigh Tuirbi, whence was it named?

"'Not difficult. Tuirbi Traghmor, the father of Goban Saer, was he who had possession in that land. He was used to throw casts of his hatchet from Tulach in Chial [*i.e.*, the hill of the hatchet] in the direction of the flood, so that the sea stopped, and did not come beyond it,'" etc.

Rendered in another manner, we have it in a poem thus :—

" Traigh Tuirbi whence the name,
According to authors I resolve,

Tuirbi of the strand (which is), superior to every strand,
The affectionate keen father of Goban,
His hatchet was used to be cast after ceasing
By this lusty large black youth,
From the yellow hill of the hatchet
Which the mighty flood touches.

" The distance he used to send his hatchet from him
The sea flowed not over it ;
Though Tuirbi was southwards in his district mighty,
It is not known of what stock his race ;
Unless he was of the goodly dark race,
Who went from Tara with the *heroic Lugh.*
Not known the race by God's decree
Of the man of the feats from Traigh Tuirbi."

Having thus far prepared my readers for a recital of the
curious circumstances which indirectly were the origin of
the boycotting of Paddy Raygan, I will close my historical
notes of Moytura, and come down to our own times and the
stirring events passing before our eyes, which will end Part
I. of this sketch.

PART II.

I found on taking charge of Castlebaldwin sub-district that
the agrarian agitation that pervaded the whole country had
not made this section any exception to the rule. The usual
amenities peculiar to the agitation had been, and to a milder
extent were, in full swing, and, indeed, I was not long in the
district before I experienced how intense and ineradicable
was the feeling on the land question.   One day I was patrolling up the side of Moytura mountain, and, having come
across a group of three men, I accosted them.   One was
evidently a farmer ; another, by his superior address, proved
to be a school-teacher ; and the third was a labourer.

" Good-morrow, men ; a fine day," I said.

" Good-morrow, kindly, sargint ; 'tis a fine day, glory be to
God. We're all right so long as He sends us the good

weather that's favourable to the craps to help us on to pay the rint," responded the farmer.

"Why, yes," I said, "so long as a man is able to meet his landlord his mind is easy."

"Ye never said a thruer thing than that, sargint, for well I know it," he continued. "There was wanst on a time whin my mind was aisy—a time whin I could lie down in my bed an' rest continted, and as aisy as the lake there below that's now sleepin' like a child in its cradle, without a cap full o' wind to disturb its rest ; but we wor in undher the good English landlord then." Here he paused as his eye wandered over the surface of the beautiful lake that lay like a mirror below in its basin, its surface unruffled by the slightest breath of wind.

"Then," I remarked, "you must have got a change of landlords."

"Oh, in throath, ye may say so, sargint, an' a bad change for us poor tinants. Whin we wor undher the good English Marquis we paid only ten shillin's an acre for that scrag o' mountain land, which was just what it was worth, but he sowld it out, an' the new man commenced risin' the rint till he ruz it to two pound an acre. Just think o' that ! From ten shillin's to two pound; our minds wasn't aisy thin, sthrivin' to pay that for it. If it was the Cornel * below there got it we wor all right, for instead o' rackrintin' a poor man, he cut it down and helped every poor sthrugglin' tinant to rise his head above wathur."

Here the teacher interposed, and, being manifestly a man of much reading, he drew the following picture :—

* Colonel Ffolliott.—The name of course at a glance bespeaks the ancient Briton and Welsh descent of the bluest blood. There was a Ffolliott title, which is now extinct. Baron Ffolliott of Ballyshannon was created in 1619, and the title became extinct in 1716. In Ireland, with the peasantry, the poet's philosophy stands better than the coronet—

> " Howe'er it be, it seems to me,
> 'Tis only noble to be good ;
> Kind hearts are more than coronets,
> And simple faith than Norman blood ".

It is exemplified in the case of Colonel Ffolliott.

"Yes, I am just now forcibly reminded of a simile once drawn from the work of an Italian poet, and applied to the case of Ireland by a great English Tribune when addressing a meeting in Dublin some years ago.   It was from a gloomy allegory by a poet, whose works were moulded in the vein of that gloomiest of Italian bards, Danté.   The author makes his hero wander on the banks of a lovely lake, dotted with verdant islands—just as Lake Arrow is there below—that seemed happy and blest by nature and climate ; to all appearance a perfect Utopia to the inhabitants, where peace and plenty reigned supreme.   There was nothing to mar the pleasing picture which the contemplation of the prospect evoked in the mind, save and except that the surface of the lake, although placid and unruffled by winds, emitted a low murmuring sound, accompanied with the appearance of a vast quantity of bubbles covering the surface of the water. Asking an explanation of this strange phenomenon, his *cicerone* or guide informed him that, although these regions were to all appearance an abode of the blest, there was a vast mass of untold suffering beneath the surface of the lake ; thousands of beings were held below in captivity by oppressors, and it was their murmurings and wailings that reached the surface in the mysterious and muffled form which attracted his notice.   I needn't explain how this picture bears on the state of Ireland ; the history of the agrarian question, past and present, is enough."

To myself the application of the allegory was plain enough, but to the farmer and his labourer it was otherwise.   Anything touching on the marvellous or superstitious has always a powerful influence on the mind of the Irish peasant, and the two unsophisticated men forgot all about the land question in contemplating the marvellous story of prisoners being held in captivity beneath a lake, and they both gazed at the teacher in wonderment, and at length the labourer asked—

"I wondher what wor they that had a howlt o' th' crathurs at the bottom, sir ?   I'd like to know, masther, av ye plaze."

For an answer he received a look of withering contempt from the teacher, who saw that his language was thrown away on barren understandings, and his chagrin was not assuaged

when the farmer turned the sublime into the ridiculous by
remarking—

"May be they wor alligaythors that had a howlt o' them.
Didn't ye say somethin' about alligaythors in the beginning
ov it, masther? I often heerd one Jack Lally say, who was
a sodger, that out in furrin parts those bastes dhrag people
undher the wather an' dhrown thim. Jack said he seen a
comrade, Tim Muldoon, held down bee one o' thim, but he
made his escape."

A look of unutterable contempt and a suppressed groan
came from the teacher, as he gave me a look which spoke as
plainly as a look could speak—"pearls before swine," and
he snapped out—"Well, if you take it that every bad landlord is an alligator, and every poor oppressed farmer a Tim
Muldoon, who is being dragged under the water, then perhaps you may take in the meaning of my—not *alligator*, but
—*allegory*. I never said a word about an alligator. However,
if you take it in this light, it'll do as well".

I could not forbear bursting into laughter at this conversation, in which the teacher, now fully alive to the ludicrous
turn his "allegory" had taken, joined heartily.

I merely adduce this incident to show the all-absorbing
feeling on the land question here as elsewhere. The usual
percentage of people had been "under protection"; but
matters had been assuaged a bit. My instructions were to
pay an odd visit when out on patrol at night to the domicile
of Paddy Raygan, who lived on the summit of Moytura
mountain. He had made an oasis in the shape of his
"little bit o' land" out of a barren waste of rocks and
mountain turf, and the trudge up the mountain was like
scaling the cliffs to an eagle's eyrie. Paddy in person was
a little thick-set, squat man, dressed in the usual provincial
costume of blue freize coat, knee breeches, and the conventional caubeen. On my first visit to Paddy's eyrie, I was
curious to learn what was the history of his boycotting, as I
had not been sufficiently long in the district to be conversant with it. As I sat at one side of the blazing turf-fire
and Paddy at the other, my men occupying the front, I drew
him out on the subject:—

"Well, Paddy, my poor man," I went on, "I see you've got your share of the trouble that's going".

"Troth, an' indeed I have, sargint avic," he responded. "But sure it wasn't mee fault; sorra's the ha'porth I done to give man, woman, or child offince, an' barrin' that her lady-ship stood to me, an' had a likin' for me, an' kep' me in my bit o' land on account ov the skiliton, I don't know afore God why I was put upon. I can only tell ye, sargint, that how it cum about was bee manes ov Misther Gladstone's Land Act o' Parlimint and the skiliton."

Now, this mysterious allusion of Paddy to Mr. Gladstone's Land Bill and a skeleton naturally aroused my curiosity. My men exchanged significant glances with me, which told me that Paddy had a story to tell of his woes, and I essayed again to draw him out :—

"Well, Pat, I believe it's a familiar saying, 'There's a skeleton in every house,' and of course you can't expect to be an exception to the rule; we all have to meet our troubles. I myself had before I came here two 'skele-tons,' and drunken ones too, sent me by the county-inspec-tor; and when I asked him why he sent them to me, he said they were sent to him, and of course he should send them to somebody else."

This had the desired effect, for the marvellous is sure to arouse the interest of the peasant. Paddy looked me full in the face, and taking the *dhudeen* he was smoking out of his mouth, he said :—

"A skiliton in every house, an' two o' thim wid you; begorra, sargint, I dunno about that. What would skilitons be doin' in every house? an' the two you had gettin' dhrunk; an' sure where could they hould dhrink iv they got id?"

"Rather strange, Pat, I admit, but nevertheless it's a fact. My 'skeletons'* had places to hold any amount of drink, and they never paid for it either."

"Begor, that was worse, sargint; but I never heerd tell ov a skiliton bein' in any house, barrin' the one I had mee-self for one night; but I know there was Jack Mulligan's ghost seen, they say, every night for years afther he died."

---

* I had two "auxiliary men," and thereby hangs a strange tale.

"Oh, then, you had a real skeleton, Paddy,"˙I said, "here in the house."

"Of coorse I had. Hadn't I Loowis o' th' Long Hand's skiliton that I found, which her ladyship an' Docther Dane, wid all their larniment, couldn't get, although they had the labourin' min diggin' away for weeks, tal ye'd think they'd turn the ould mountain inside out. They wor three days at the *caurawn* (*cairn*) but got nothin' but a goold ornamint in it. Sure I found his stone coffin, an' his skiliton, an' armour, and helmit, an' swoord, an' his goold breast-plate, an' all."

And thereby hangs a tale to Paddy's communication, the main facts and surroundings of which I gleaned, not only from Paddy, but various other channels, the origin of which was

AN EXTRAORDINARY WAGER.

The estate of which the historic townland of Moytura (*Magh Tuireadh*) forms a part, had been, it would appear, owned by an English Marquis, who was a true specimen of the good old English gentleman of the Sir Roger De Coverley type, kind and considerate to his tenants, and particularly so to his Irish tenants. But, unluckily for them, he sold out his Irish property, and a change of owners brought a change of *régime*. The rents that had been at their minimum went up by stages to their maximum in a short space of time, with the inevitable result of a brisk crop of evictions for non-payment of rent. To add to the gloomy days the tenants had fallen upon, the well-intentioned but misused Land Act of '70-'71 gave an impetus to the eviction phase of the land question.

Now, her ladyship, the better half of the new lord of the soil of Moytura, was a bit of a *savant* in her way, and was fairly versed in ancient Irish history in its labyrinthine mazes. She was wont to enter into learned discussions upon disputed historical questions, and used to wax so warm in supporting her views and arguments, that she invariably ended the dispute by offering to lay a large wager, to be decided by arbitration, or the production of some *prima facie* evidence

that she was right.   It came about, so the story goes, that
she had a very lengthened disquisition on the battle of *Magh-
Tuireadh* with a *savant* of London, who happened to be of
the Jewish persuasion, and enormously rich.   The question
at issue, it would appear, was as to where Lugh Lamfhada
fell, her ladyship contending that he was killed at the second
battle of *Magh-Tuireadh*, her antagonist stoutly holding to
the contrary.   With her usual impetuosity, her ladyship
challenged the rich Jew to a wager for a large amount of
money that she would prove herself right, by finding the
tomb of *Lugh Lamfhada* in Moytura, on her husband's
estate, and bring to London the skeleton, with any relic,
such as his armour, helmet, sword, etc.   She also contended
that Lewy of the Long Hand was a giant, in accordance
with the "Historic Tales," which represent him as such.
The Jew took up as hotly her ladyship's gage in the shape
of the money-wager, and the arbitrators and spectators waited
with curiosity and interest the outcome of the singular com-
pact.   Lady T—— forthwith quitted London for Ireland.
When there, she repaired to the neighbourhood of Moytura
Mountain, and took up her residence at a neighbouring
gentleman's mansion.   She then procured the aid of the
eminent T. N. Deane, Esq., R.H.A., of Dublin, who, if I
mistake not, has something to do with the ancient monuments and remains of Ireland ; and they, with the service of
a gang of labourers, made a thorough search through the
mountain, excavating here and there for weeks to no avail.
There is a cairn on the mountain, and great hopes were
entertained that the tomb of the giant-hero would be found
in it ; but after herculean labour being expended in excavating beneath it, nothing but a gold or silver ancient Irish
ornament was found.   Her ladyship had taken Paddy Raygan into her confidence, and constituted him her guide
through the mountain, and had promised him her powerful
aid in keeping him from being evicted by his lordship, who
seemed a very matter-of-fact sort of nobleman.   "Regan,"
she would say, "I'll keep you in your holding, no matter
what is said to the contrary, if you lead me to where I'll find
Lewy of the Long Hand's tomb."

Now these hopes and promises inspired Paddy with great zeal in her ladyship's cause, and he paid strict attention to everything she or Mr. Deane said ; he gleaned a lot of fragments of historical lore which her ladyship recited from the "Historical Tales" about Lugh's courtship, and how he came to have a long hand, or rather arm, and told him (Paddy) of Nuadhat of the Silver Hand, and Balor of the Evil Eye, etc., which Paddy jumbled up in a very extraordinary manner afterwards, when telling it his own way. One day, when all hopes of finding Lugh's tomb were abandoned, Lady T—— and Mr. Deane took refuge in Paddy's cabin from a heavy shower of rain. When they were leaving it, and were about a stone's-throw from Paddy's cabin door, something beneath their feet attracted the attention of Mr. Deane. It had some appearance of large flag-like stones, arranged as if by design, and he pointed it out to her ladyship, who only laughed at him for being so silly, as she said, to imagine that Lugh would be entombed in such a place, without a cairn or mark. Mr. Deane, notwithstanding, urged on her the advisability of excavating there, but to no use, and that day ended their operations. Mr. Deane returned to Dublin, and Lady T—— discharged her labourers, and gave up as lost her wager of no less, I am told, than £10,000.

Now Paddy, as I have stated, observed carefully everything said and done by Lady T—— and Mr. Deane, and he noted the spot which Mr. Deane pointed out. Next day, when left alone, he brought his spade and crow-bar, and commenced excavating round the stones, which, when freed from the earth that partially covered them, proved to be a series of great flags, evidently covering a cavity. On this discovery, Paddy's excitement was intense, for a number of cogent and deeply interesting motives urged him on to move heaven and earth to succeed in discovering the object of her ladyship's quest. In the first place, the hope of a money-reward which she had promised him ; secondly, he expected to find some treasure buried with Lugh which he meant to keep for himself ; and her ladyship often speaking of Nuadhat of the Silver Hand, he somehow identified that monarch as one and the same person as Lugh Longhanded, so that he expected to find a silver hand as well as a long hand ; then, lastly, the potent factor of securing immunity from the fate which overtook hundreds, by reason of the Compensation for Disturbance Bill becoming law, namely, eviction or the "lease". Can we wonder then that Paddy Raygan was excited on his discovery, or that he flung down his crow-bar and rushed in to tell Molly, his wife, of his expected discovery, just as of old Archimedes rushed out of his bath, shouting "Eureka !" "Arrah, Molly *asthore*, our sowls to glory, but av I haven't found it mee name's not Paddy Raygan. Come out, *avic machree*, an' gi'e me a helpin' hand, for I'm not able to lift the shtones that's coverin' id."

And Paddy and his better-half repaired to the spot, and with considerable difficulty lifted one of the great flags, which revealed a long chamber beneath, the walls of which were great stones like those covering it.   Paddy then went on his hands and knees and peered down into the cavity, and to his wondering gaze there was revealed, after a sleep of centuries, the relics of the *Tuatha-de-Danaan* hero, the redoubtable *Lugh Lamfhada*. A helmet encased the skull of the skeleton, and a cuirass or breast-plate lay on the breast ; a sword rested by its left side, and fragments and remnants of armour, eaten and decayed with the rust of ages, lay around.   There was no silver hand or treasure, to Paddy's disappointment ; but what most impressed him with awe and wonder was an enormous tooth in the jaw of the skeleton ; and here I deem it proper to let Paddy himself give some account of the transaction.

"Well ye see, sargint, her ladyship tould me how Looey o' th' Long Hand was a joint (*giant*), an' how he kem to have a long arm was this : He heerd tell ov a jointess that was a very purty gerl wid a fortune, an' he wint to ax her father to give her to 'im, but this ould joint didn't think Looey good enough for his daughter, an' axed him how daar he have th' impidence to cum lookin' for his daughther, for a mane spalpeen like him, an' to go home about his business.

"'Bad luck to yer impidence ye ould buddhach,' says Looey, 'I'm as good as ever ye wor, ye ould boccach o' th' divil,' says he, ' an' I'll have her now in spite o' ye. Whin yer not goin' to give her to me bee fair manes, I'll get her be foul manes,' says he, an' wid that he left the joint's castle. Well, then, th' ould joint locked his daughther up in a top room ov his castle, for he knew she was favourable to Looey. But Looey kem one night an' gev a whistle which she knew, an' she put her head out o' th' windy, an' said, ' I'll go wid ye, Looey, av ye get me down '.

" ' Och, mavourneen,' says Looey, ' the windy is very high an' how could I get ye down, mee darlint, widout a laddher ? '

" ' Didn't yer mother ever larn ye th' art o' wishin' ? ' says she.

" ' No, avic,' says he.

" ' Well then,' says she, ' put yer thumb in yer mouth an' wish three times for anything, an' ye'll get id.'

" Well, Looey put his thumb in his mouth an' wished three times that his arm was long enough to raitch up to the joint's daughther, when, mee jule an' darlint, his right arm grew so long that he raitched id up, an' lifted the gerl down out o' the windy, an' she run away wid 'im ; an' the ould joint, her father, followed them, an' nearly cotch them sleepin' on a bag o' sand on the saeshore, an' that's how he kem to have a long hand. But, begor, I watched what Docther Dane said more than her ladyship, for I knew he was a knowin' man an' she only aimin' at bein' cliver. ' Raggan,' says she, I'll keep ye in yer howldin', no matther who goes out, av ye lade me to where I'll find Looey o' th' Long Hand's grave. Don't let me be worsted bee a Lundon Jew,' says she ; ' ye know th' ould Irish blood's in me.' ' I'll do mee best, mee lady,' says I. ' So ye may be sure, sargint, I was sky high wid rejoicement whin I found Looey's grave, an' prayed for Docther Dane, for ye see his lordship was poppin' thim out on account of Misther Gladstone's Act o' Parliament."

So far, dear reader, for Paddy's extraordinary versions and views of matters and things ; but to return to his action at the tomb of Lugh Lamfhada. He got down into the vault and got the skeleton out, with the armour, helmet, and sword, and, as it was rather late, he waited till next morning to take his precious trophy to Lady T——, who stopped for a day or two at her temporary abode before she started home. Next day he started with the vertebræ and small bones, sword, helmet, and breastplate, in a bag on his back ; the skull, which he was apprehensive might be crushed in the bag, he tied carefully up in a threepenny hankerchief, and the arm, thigh, and leg bones tied in a bundle under his arm. I think I have endeavoured to establish a theory that nothing can occur in Ireland without its comic side ; and grim and lugubrious as Paddy's burthen and mission were that day, it could not pass off without its comic episode. He chanced to meet Sergeant Doolin in charge of a neighbouring barrack, a very zealous and strict officer in the discharge of his duty, especially on all matters sanitary. He had been visiting some place where cattle disease (*pleuropneumonia*) was reported to be ; and any one conversant with official life well knows what strictness is enforced in such cases, and how circular after circular is issued on the matter.

The sergeant, seing the bones under Paddy's arm, imagined them the bones of some animal, they were so large ; and thinking they might carry the infection with them, he stopped Paddy to question him on the matter—

" Hollo ! Paddy Raygan, where did you get these bones, or where are you goin' with them ? " he asked.

" Wid all rispects for you, Sargint Doolin," replied Paddy, " it's none o' yer business where I got thim or where I'm goin' wid thim aither."

" I'll let you see it is my business and my duty too," rejoined the sergeant tartly ; " you, nor any one else will be allowed to be hawkin' bones about the counthry spreadin' infection and disease, so give me up these bones till I have them berrid ; I suppose ye have another lot in the bag."

" No matther what's in or out o' th' bag, I tell ye agin, Sargint Doolin, it's none o' yer business to stop me an' me bones."

" If you don't give me up these bones until I have them berrid," reiterated the sergeant, " I'll have you arrested under the sanitary laws. Is it in a churchyard ye got them ? or is it a rag-an'-bone man you've turned out ? "

" I tell ye agin," said Paddy firmly, " that I'll not give up my bones to man or morthial, while there's life in mee body, tal I give them up to her ladyship. D'ye want me to be put out o' my land? an' these bones is the only thing that'll save me. Ain't they puttin' them out accordin' to Misther Gladstone's act o' parliament, an' didn't her ladyship tell me if I got Lewis o' th' Long Hand's bones, she'd keep me in mee howldin'. An' sure, be manes ov Docther Dane, I got them where he said they wor. Och, mee jewel and darlint, av her ladyship heerd I got thim an' gev thim to anyone else, an' she havin' to lose her bet wid the London Jew, out I'd go, nothin' id save me."

Now, this extraordinary and mysterious speech of Paddy was simply Greek to Sergeant Doolin, for he had not the remotest idea of its meaning; he had heard nothing of the search of Lady T——, and the rambling statement in which were jumbled together in a most, to him, inexplicable manner, "her ladyship"—"put out of his land"—"bones to save him from eviction"—"Mr. Gladstone's Land Act"—"Lewis of the Long Hand"—"Doctor Deane"—"a bet with a London Jew"—together with his determined attitude, impressed the sergeant with the belief that Paddy Raygan was mad, and that his strange language was simply the incoherent mutterings and ravings of a lunatic. Feeling that responsibility devolved upon him to secure Paddy, he conveyed an "ultimatum" to him thus:—

"I tell ye what it is, Raygan, I can't allow you, under such suspicious circumstances, to go wherever yer goin'; so you must come with me."

"I tell ye agin, Sargint Doolin, wanst for all," said Paddy, "I'll not give up the bones or go wid ye aither, barrin' I'm a corp, for I might as well be dead as put out o' mee land, so I might as well die wan way as another; so let me pass wid mee bones, an' av ye have anything agin me, ye can shue me in the law afterwards."

Now, of all men, Sergeant Doolin hated ridiculous phrases touching his profession, and this last idiom of Paddy, "shue me in the law," raised his (the sergeant's) ire, and he imitated Paddy—"shue ye in the la-a-w".

"D'ye think that I'm a laygal shoemaker that I have to

make a pair of laygal shoes for ye?   I tell ye now, I'll have
no more humbuggin', only ye'll come with me."

Paddy now seeing the sergeant making a move towards
him stepped back, and laying the bag and skull on the
ground, he whipped one of the great leg bones out of the
·bundle under his arm, and holding it as a shillelagh, he
stood on the defensive, and menacing the sergeant with the
bone, he said, having manifestly waxed desperate—

"I tell ye what it is, Sargint Doolin, I'll not give in tal
I'm kilt, for I'll sthrek ye wid this bone av ye lay hands on
me, an' I advise ye not to put an me to sthrek ye, for ye'll
nivir recover av ye get a blow o' this bone.   It's the thigh-
bone o' Lewis o' th' Long Hand, an' her ladyship says no
man ivir recovered that he sthruck, for there's vinom in the
bone ov 'im still.   An' av ye want to berry Lewis's skiliton,
go down to her ladyship an' ax her about it.   She's stoppin'
there below, only a couple o' miles away at Mr. ——; for I
tell ye ye'll have to kill me afore I'll go or give up the bones,
an' thin id's not one skiliton ye'll have to berry, but three o'
them."

Now, it will be noted that this feat of burying three skele-
tons, namely, the sergeant's own when killed by Paddy,
Paddy's when killed by the sergeant, and Lugh Lamfhada's
was a very unprecedented one indeed, which Paddy warned
the sergeant he would have to perform.

The sergeant, seeing the menacing attitude taken up by
Paddy, instinctively laid his hand on his sword, for, not
being free from the superstition of his countrymen, he did
not relish a blow from a dead man's bone administered by
a madman, and in his turn stood on the defensive.   Paddy
and he eyed each other for some minutes, waiting which
should make the attack.   Now Paddy, seeing a struggle for
life or death at hand, in his anxiety for the safety of his
precious "organic remains," stooped down and lifted the
bag, bones, and skull into the ditch, so that they would not
be trampled to smithereens in the struggle, and in so doing
the skull rolled out of the threepenny handkerchief.   For
the first time Sergeant Doolin laid eyes on the skull of the
Tuatha-de-Danaan hero, and it turned the tide of battle in

Paddy's favour. That one look at that awful skull, with the terrible tooth which excited Paddy's awe and wonder, was enough for Sergeant Doolin. All the superstition of his race rose to the surface in his mind, and he turned as pale as a sheet and beat a hasty retreat from the scene, leaving Paddy monarch of all he surveyed. Paddy looked after him as his retreating form grew small by degrees, and he chuckled, " Begorra, he's gone. That ye may never come back, an' a bottle o' moss av we never seen ye; ye're no grate loss, Misther Busybody Doolin. Bad win' to me but the skull frikened him. More power to ye, Lewis avic; id's not the first ye frikened," and he patted the skull; and having got the bones and bag to rights again, he pursued the tenor of his way towards Lady T——'s temporary abode, on which journey we will leave him for a while and return to Sergeant Doolin.

That efficient officer soliloquised as well as Paddy Raygan. " Well, that bates out all ever crossed me. Raygan is mad, ragin' mad. It must be that they're puttin' him out of his land, and it has set him mad. But where did he get the bones ? I didn't think they were human bones till I seen the skull, an' such an awful skull ; " here the sergeant shuddered and ejaculated, " Lord save us ! I wonder was it in Ballindoon graveyard he dug them up ? There'll be a job now bringin' him off to the asylum. But where is he facin' now, I wonder. He imagines he's going to Lady T——, an' that she'll keep him from eviction for a lot of dead men's bones. Well, if that's not lunacy my name's not Doolin. I wonder is his townland in my district. No, begob, it's in Mickey's ; I've nothin' to do with him ; Moytura is in Castlebaldwin sub-district. I'll send word to Mickey about him," and here the sergeant chuckled at the discovery that trouble devolved on someone else regarding Paddy Raygan ; and he ceased his soliloquising as he perceived he was meeting a neighbouring man, who proved to be Tim Byron, whom I have introduced to the reader before. " Here's Tim Byron, and I'll ask him if he knows anything about Raygan," was the sergeant's last thought, and as Tim approached the sergeant accosted him—

"Good morning, Tim ; a fine day ".

"Good morning kindly, sergeant," responded Tim ; " 'tis a fine day, glory be to God."

"Tell me, Tim, d'ye know anything about Paddy Raygan of the hill above ?   I met him a while ago an' he had a lot o' bones an' a skull an' somethin' in a bag, an' faith I thought he was mad."

"Oh, then," says Tim, " ye never made a greater mistake. Divil a one ov him mad ; he knows what he's about ; let Raygan out ; I warrant ye ye'll not see him put out ov his land.   Sure didn't he find the whole lot Lady T—— was diggin' through the mountain for wid twenty men—sum owld king or another that was berrid there ; an' hasn't he the goold plates, an' armour, an' swoord an' all ?   Oh, divil a wink av Raygan."

Now here was a revelation to Sergeant Doolin.   The whole truth flashed on him, that in the bag Paddy had was the treasure trove, and his official mind grasped the fact at once, that great credit awaited him if he got possession of it, and made an official report regarding it, and he said to Tim—

"Tim, yer sowl to glory, will ye run afther Raygan and tell him I'll give him five pounds for the bones ; five pounds, mind ye ! an' if ye get them for me we'll have a drop over it below at Pat's, an' I won't forget ye."

"Begor, that I will, an' no mistake," said Tim, who in anticipation of his reward, ran after Paddy at top speed, and when in sight of him he kept shouting—

"Hello ! Paddy ! Misther Raygan ! Paddy, yer sowl, howld an.   The sargint'll give ye five pounds for the bones."

When he got near enough to Paddy, that individual replied—"Arrah now, Tim Byron, d'ye think I'm mad or dhrunk ?   D'ye want me to be put out o' mee land?   I'll give the bones up to nobody but her ladyship."

And so Tim's mission failed, and as he looked after Paddy' he muttered—"Musha, bad luck t'ye, ye owld Shrumahawn ; cock ye up wid five pounds," and he went back to report his failure to the sergeant, who said—" Well, we can't help him.   I'd soon make him give them up, only ye tell me that Lady T—— is concerned in it ; but, come back an' we'll have the drink all the same."

Great was the delight of Lady T—— when Paddy Raygan disclosed his treasures to her. To use Paddy's own words she "danced like a fairy and handled the bones like a docther," and gave Paddy a money reward of five shillings ! She got a box made and packed them carefully up, and took them away to London, and triumphantly carried off her wager of £10,000 from the Jew-Crœsus. The skeleton, I understand, now ornaments a London museum.

It will not be wondered at that Paddy was first favourite on the estate with the T—— family, which naturally focussed jealousy and suspicion on him by the other tenants ; and when, in some years after, boycotting was resorted to, poor Paddy came under the ban, the origin of all, as he said, was "the skiliton and Mr. Gladstone's Land Act".

However, he always alludes to one unpleasant fact, which is the ridiculously small reward Lady T—— gave him, and he makes an ugly comparison between her and Sergeant Doolin,. "Begorra, the quolity, God bless them, think a dale o' money. Lady T—— gave me five shillin's, and Sergeant Doolin offered me five pound."

I measured the vault and, if my memory serves me, it was fourteen feet in length, and Paddy told me the skeleton was in proportion to this length, which would go to prove the " Historical Tales " as correct in describing men as of giant proportions in those times. But the secret as to who *really was* exhumed by Paddy Raygan can never be found out. I had an idea that it may be Balor of the Evil Eye, which is more probable than that it was *Lugh Lamfhada.*

A curious circumstance was told me by Paddy. He had a good healthy goat which he put down into the vault one night for shelter, and in the morning the animal was found dead.